ONE HUNDRED YEARS OF TANNER

BOOK 19 OF THE TANNER SERIES

REMINGTON KANE

Year Zero

INTRODUCTION

ONE HUNDRED YEARS OF TANNER – A
TANNER NOVEL – BOOK 19

During a visit to see Spenser in Wyoming, Tanner and
Spenser discuss the first Tanner.

And after Spenser is contacted by a client, Tanner and
Romeo tag along to lend a hand.

ACKNOWLEDGMENTS

I write for you.

—Remington Kane

THIS IS NOT A WORK OF HISTORICAL FACT
THIS IS A RECORD OF HISTORICAL FICTION

1

GREETINGS & SALUTATIONS

CODY, WYOMING – PRESENT DAY

Sara smiled as she watched Tanner greet his mentor, Spenser Hawke, with a heartfelt hug. They were in the open foyer of Spenser's home, beyond which lay the living room. Tanner had grown more relaxed since they'd left the airport and Sara realized that for Tanner, Wyoming was home.

Spenser was handsome, and younger than Sara had expected him to be. He was maybe a hair taller than Tanner and just as fit. His one good eye studied her as he sent Sara a smile in greeting. When he released Tanner from their hug, he extended a hand toward her.

"My name is Spenser. It's good to meet you, Sara. I've heard a lot about you."

Sara sighed. "I assume that not all of it was good."

"No, not in the earlier discussions concerning you, but I can't wait to get to know you better. Anyone that can give

Cody here a run for his money must be an interesting person."

"As is anyone who has been a Tanner," Sara said. "And it's a pleasure to meet you too."

Spenser's fiancée, Amy, was standing by and taking in the scene. There was a smile on her lips, but Sara saw that Amy was scrutinizing her. She understood why. Amy had only known Tanner with Alexa, and Amy and Alexa had become friends. Seeing Tanner with another woman had to be an adjustment, especially since she was a woman who had tried to kill Tanner on more than one occasion.

"My name is Amy."

Sara shook Amy's extended hand. "Sara Blake, it's nice to meet you."

A voice shouted from the top of the staircase. "Bro!"

It was Romeo. He and his family had traveled to Wyoming from their home in Indonesia. He was dressed in jeans and a black sleeveless T-shirt, which displayed the many tattoos on his arms. Instead of walking down the stairs, Romeo slid down the banister, landed in a graceful crouch, then all but tackled Tanner as he embraced him in a bear hug.

Two more figures appeared at the top of the stairs. When Sara saw the smaller of the two, an involuntary sound of, "Ooohh," escaped her lips.

Romeo's wife, Nadya, came down the stairs holding their infant daughter, Florentina. Florentina looked like a little angel wrapped inside her pink cotton gown. She had Nadya's dark hair and amber eyes combined with Romeo's light skin.

As Sara moved past Romeo, she greeted him with a peck on the cheek while giving his hand a squeeze. She kissed Nadya as well, then looked down in wonder at the baby. "She's so beautiful, Nadya."

"Would you like to hold her?"

Sara grinned, said "Yes," and as she held the infant in her arms, her face seemed to glow. Little Florentina gazed up with a smile as Sara spoke to her in baby talk.

Romeo nudged Tanner in the ribs. "Uh-oh, Bro, Sara's getting the mommy fever."

Sara turned and smiled at Romeo. "I do want children someday, but not now."

TANNER AND SARA SETTLED IN THEIR ROOM, SHOWERED, then joined everyone else, who were seated outside on the patio, where Spenser was manning a grill.

As Sara spoke to Spenser, Amy asked Tanner about Alexa.

"I really thought you two would last," Amy said.

"I did too, but it turned out that Alexa and I saw the future differently."

"You didn't want to get married, have children?"

"I can see that happening someday, but Alexa also wanted me to stop being Tanner. I don't want to stop being Tanner."

Amy looked over her shoulder at Sara. "And this Sara, she's all right with that?"

An amused look came over Tanner as he answered. "Sara knows me better than almost anyone, so yes, she understands me and is okay with what I do."

"Did she really try to kill you, Cody?"

"Several times, and I tried to kill her as well."

Amy looked over at Sara again. "She must be tougher than she looks."

"You don't know the half," Tanner said.

3

∾

At the grill, Sara and Spenser talked about Tanner.

"Tanner said he owes you his life, Spenser."

"It's true. I only wish I could have saved his family as well."

"He's less intense around you and Romeo, and that's because Tanner thinks of you two as his family."

Spenser studied Sara. "Do you ever call him Cody, or only Tanner?"

"I've never called him Cody, but I do call him Thomas when necessary, which is the alias he's living under in New York City, Thomas Myers."

Spenser laughed. "I've used so many aliases over the years that I can't even remember them all. And for a long time, Cody went by the name of Xavier, which is the name Nadya likes to call him."

"Why does she still call him by that name?"

Spenser shrugged. "That was the name he was using when they met. She was just a child, but then, Cody and Romeo were only a few years older than she was."

Sara looked over and saw that Tanner and Amy were talking with Romeo and Nadya. "Tanner and Romeo once worked together, I mean, as hit men?"

Spenser nodded. "I had trained them as well as I could, and they were both young and ready to prove themselves."

"Prove themselves to you, to see which of them would be the next Tanner?"

"Not really. Romeo knew early on that Cody was better than he was, and that he wanted to be a Tanner more than anything. On the other hand, Romeo was just after adventure, and they sure did get plenty of that."

"How long did they work together?"

"For years, and then I lost my eye and… a new Tanner was born, Tanner Seven."

"When I was with the F.B.I., my superiors thought the Tanner legend was just a myth. They admitted that there were assassins using the name Tanner, but they thought you were all unrelated, and just using the name to gain a reputation. I believed that was the case even after tracking Tanner for most of a year."

"No, there have only been seven of us, and as a matter of fact, we've been around a hundred years."

"The first Tanner, what was he like?" Sara asked.

Spenser smiled as he flipped a burger. "I never met him. Just how old do you think I am?"

Sara laughed. "Tanner said that there were records you kept."

"It's called the Book of Tanner, and yes, our history is recorded in it."

"All one hundred years?"

"Yes, but Cody still has to add to it. His victory over Maurice Scallato will be a highlight to the book."

"The first Tanner, was Tanner his surname? And why did he become a hit man?"

"Ah, now that's quite a story," Spenser said.

5

2

KEANE O'CONNELL

CHICAGO, ILLINOIS, NOVEMBER 1916

DAVIN O'CONNELL BREATHED IN A SERIES OF GASPS, AS THE illness that was taking his life ate at his vitality. Seated at bedside was Davin's older brother, Keane O'Connell, who attempted to give his brother whatever comfort he could during his last days.

They were in the basement of a rooming house, and the dust-covered discards of past tenants were stacked all around them. Above them, the other tenants went about their business. Because it was a Sunday, many were at home, but during the week, most of the men worked down at the docks.

Keane paid their landlord extra to use the basement for a makeshift hospital room, with the condition that none of the other tenants would encounter Davin, who was contagious. There was a toilet and a sink in a corner, but you had to run a bucket of water down the toilet to get rid of the waste, since the water tank had been broken and never replaced. The previous owner of the building once had plans to turn the basement into an apartment, but he had never followed through on them.

Davin hated hospitals and had begged Keane not to place him in one of the wards where he would die as a number on a chart. Keane had agreed but shocked his brother by remaining at his side.

The red-headed Davin was dying of consumption, also known as tuberculosis. He'd been coughing up blood, and both Davin and Keane knew that the disease had progressed rapidly over the past weeks.

"Leave me down here alone, Keane," Davin had begged, but Keane waved away his brother's concerns. In truth, he didn't care if he contracted the disease or not.

Keane O'Connell was thirty-two. His wife had died back in Ireland after giving birth to their only child, a son, while the baby died three days later.

Davin was the last member of Keane's family. Once he passed away, Keane would be alone in a strange country. He had only made plans to move to America at his wife's request. She had wanted their child to be raised there. As his only living kin, Davin had decided to join his brother in the new world and made arrangements for passage on a ship.

At the time, they had no idea that they would take the voyage in part as a way to flee painful memories.

Keane and Davin had left Ireland after being involved in what was being called the Easter Rising.

The Irish Republicans fought to establish an independent Ireland while the United Kingdom was preoccupied with fighting in the First World War. The British responded with immense force and the fighting in Dublin lasted only six days before the rising was suppressed.

Keane and Davin had fought hard in street battles, but it was the elder brother, Keane, who revealed a penchant for killing. During those six days, Keane O'Connell had killed so many men that he'd lost count of them. His only regret was that he hadn't killed more.

Keane was an educated man and had worked as a history teacher. He enjoyed reading about history and never tired of learning, but he was passionate about his former homeland and had fought in vain to achieve its independence.

Davin chuckled at a memory, but it triggered a coughing spell. He turned his head away from his brother, as he attempted to shield him from his infectious breath. Keane didn't care whether he caught the disease or not, for once Davin was gone, he'd have no reason to live.

"What made you laugh?" Keane asked. His Irish accent was lyrical.

Davin's voice carried the same tone but was rougher because of his disease. "I was thinking of you. You're a gentle man, Brother, but Lordy, how you killed when the fighting was on. If we'd had more like you, we'd have won the rebellion."

"We both fought well. If not for the artillery they used against us, we'd have had a fine chance at victory."

"So many of our fellows were arrested and executed. I never thought we'd be allowed to sail here," Davin said.

"We were fortunate that we had made our plans to leave before the rebellion and blessed that no one gave up our names to the British."

"You should join the army when the money runs out. The Americans aren't in the war and have no reason to join the fighting."

"I'll think about it," Keane said. "But we still have enough to last us for months."

Keane and Davin had come across a group of British soldiers who'd been looting a Dublin bank after an artillery shell had collapsed its roof and a wall that contained the safe. Most of the money burned in the resulting fire, but after killing the soldiers, the two brothers had left the scene with an unexpected supply of cash. It was enough so that Keane could tend to his brother without needing to work. Although they'd had a good sum of money, they had traveled in steerage, as most of the other immigrants did. The thin gruel served aboard ship disgusted Keane. When he arrived in America, he vowed never to eat oatmeal again.

Davin coughed violently, and for nearly a minute. When he removed the cloth he'd held against Davin's mouth, it was covered in blood. Keane closed his eyes against the sting of tears. His little brother was dying, and there was every reason to believe that he too would succumb to the disease.

"One good thing about dying," Davin said in a raspy voice. "I'll soon be with those who went before me."

Keane nodded, although he had no clue what to expect after death. He assumed it would be no different than life, in that you never knew what lay in store for you.

He reached out, gripped his brother's clammy hand, and held on to it, as a tear leaked and ran down his cheek.

3

OPPORTUNITY ARISES

CHICAGO, ILLINOIS, MARCH 1917

KEANE O'CONNELL WATCHED FROM THE WORKSHOP FLOOR as four young hoodlums crowded around his boss, Sid Hershel.

The office in the middle of the factory had glass windows on three sides, but they were so dirty that they could scarcely be seen through. However, someone had cleaned a circle of glass for a view of the workshop, and it was through this clear spot of window that Keane gazed upon the scene in the office.

Davin had died in December, and Keane had buried him in a proper Catholic cemetery. It had taken a good chunk of his remaining money and he had to find work by February.

The fact that he had not followed Davin into the grave surprised O'Connell, but he had never developed so much as a cough. He had always been a hardy soul, but

11

consumption had claimed so many that he thought it amazing he had not contracted the illness.

He was doing manual labor and being paid slave wages but had been unable to find a job as a teacher. The work was hard, conditions poor, and he was often called by the racial slurs of Mick or Paddy. Unlike his freckled brother who'd had red hair and a light complexion, O'Connell had dark hair, but his Irish accent gave away his roots every time.

Slow to anger over petty concerns and needing a job, O'Connell let the slurs roll off his back. Laying hands upon him was another matter. He had beaten two men in a bar brawl a week earlier, after one of them had pushed him.

In his place of work, he was a lone Irishman, as most of the other workers were Italian, along with a few Germans. His fellow workers left him alone and he returned the favor.

Inside the office, one of the punks shoved O'Connell's boss backwards. Sid Hershel maintained his balance, but not his dignity, and tears wet his bearded cheeks. Another of the punks punched Hershel in the stomach, then shouted at him.

"This time tomorrow… or else, you hear?"

The punk's accent was pure Cockney, which made O'Connell dislike him immediately.

Along one wall of the office was a rack of brown leather jackets. They were a new product that Hershel was developing, as he hoped to get a lucrative contract with the military. The English punk started handing them out to his companions while also taking one for himself.

The punks left the office and marched past O'Connell as if they owned the place. O'Connell glanced back inside the office and saw Hershel seated at the desk with his head in his hands.

The man has a problem, O'Connell thought, and wondered how Sid Hershel would solve it.

O'CONNELL LEFT WORK THAT EVENING AND STROLLED across the street to where a row of new homes was being erected. The homes were just wooden frames and still lacked flooring, but they all had thick planks laid across the floor beams for the workers to walk on as they were building. O'Connell sat on one of the planks and let his legs dangle as he waited for his boss to lock up for the night.

As he sat there, O'Connell smoked his pipe and pondered what Hershel would do. To his way of thinking, Sid Hershel had three choices. He could give in to the thugs threatening him, he could involve the police, or he could find help in dealing with the problem.

When Sid Hershel closed for the day and headed toward the docks, O'Connell was certain that Hershel had chosen to seek help outside the law. He was right, and Hershel was soon huddled in the corner of a bar with two of the largest men O'Connell had ever seen.

At one point, O'Connell moved closer and was able to catch a snatch of their conversation. He had heard the big men speaking in low tones, and both had German accents.

"We'll do it," said one of the men, while the other had nodded while saying. "They'll just disappear."

A few moments after that, Sid Hershel passed one of the brutes a wad of bills. With their business concluded, the men separated as they left the bar.

O'Connell placed his empty shot glass on the bar and followed the Germans.

THE GERMANS WALKED DOWN MAXWELL STREET, AND AS they moved along they pointed out the dark faces among the crowds. The Negroes were coming up from the Southern states in greater numbers and that caused concern for many.

As an Irishman who'd been treated like a minority in his own country, O'Connell wished the Negroes luck in carving out a spot for themselves. He knew what it felt like to be marginalized in the country in which you were born.

O'Connell saw the Germans move down an alleyway that took them over to a dead-end street. The street was a dead-end because a wooden building had collapsed across it. Given the look of the rubble, the building had tumbled down decades earlier and just never been carted away.

Everything in the area looked old and vacant, but there was the glow of a fire coming from a boarded-up house.

O'Connell hung back in the shadows and watched the Germans. The two brutes were fools. They stood out in the open and stared across at the home where the fire glow came from. If anyone inside was looking out, they would know their intentions.

The Germans split up, as one man lumbered up the front steps, while his companion moved toward the back of the home. They had both taken out guns, a pair of stubby revolvers that looked like toys in their massive hands.

When a loud whistling sound came from the rear of the home, the German on the porch kicked in the front door and entered. Shouts came from inside, and O'Connell heard the distinct cadence of cockney among the raised voices. To his surprise, no gunshots echoed in the house, but he did hear a great struggle.

One of the Germans appeared at the front door. It was the man who had slipped around the rear of the home. His face was red, and his hands were at his own throat, as he attempted in vain to free the wire garrote that was killing him.

The German was pulled back inside the house as the shouting lessened, then, a foot kicked the front door closed. However, a gap remained between the door and its damaged frame and O'Connell saw a face peeking out at the street. O'Connell stayed still, knowing that he was hidden among deep shadows and couldn't be seen.

Laughter drifted out of the house as the punks discovered the money Sid Hershel had given the brutes. The laughter was followed by a cry of pain, then a spate of words spoken with a guttural German accent. A name was uttered, the name of Sid Hershel.

O'Connell left the area unseen and headed back the way he'd come, knowing he had an opportunity to make some real money. Sid Hershel had only made his problem worse. He would be frightened and desperate. But that was good, because he'd have more incentive than ever to solve his problem.

Keane O'Connell could do that for him, for he had a knack for killing.

4

WORK MORE SUITED FOR A MAN

As he suspected he would, O'Connell found that Sid Hershel had returned to his place of business to await word from the Germans he'd hired to kill the punks harassing him. The shop floor was in darkness, but a light glowed in the office. O'Connell had left a window unlatched earlier so that he'd have a way inside if needed. He used it, edged closer to the office door, and peeked inside.

Hershel was bent over with his back to the door as he opened a floor safe. O'Connell's eyes grew wide when he saw the stacks of bills inside. Along with the money was a gun.

O'Connell marched inside the office just as Hershel was reaching for the weapon. At the sound of his footsteps, Hershel squawked in fear and grabbed for the revolver. O'Connell grabbed his boss's hand as it came around holding the weapon. A slight bit of pressure on a nerve at Hershel's wrist caused him to release the gun, and it tumbled onto the top of the desk.

O'Connell claimed the gun with one hand, even as he

shoved Sid Hershel into his office chair. The look of fear on Hershel's face changed into one of recognition, and he pointed at O'Connell.

"You work for me."

"I did, but I won't after tonight."

Hershel stared at O'Connell, then shook his head. "I don't remember your name."

"A man like you wouldn't. You treat your workers like shite."

Hershel's face reddened in anger. "I gave you and the other men jobs, and I pay well too."

"You pay no more than you have to, which is fine, but it's still a pittance."

Hershel glanced back at his open safe. "Is that why you're robbing me?"

"I'm no thief, but I have killed before, and I'll kill again, but it will cost you dearly."

"What are you talking about?"

"Those Germans you hired are dead, Hershel. The four punks you sent them to kill were too much for them."

Sid Hershel's face went white at that news, and he trembled. He reached into a bottom drawer. O'Connell brought the gun up, expecting to see Hershel bring out another weapon, but instead, it was a glass, along with a brown bottle of whiskey named Old Underoof.

Sid Hershel downed half a glass of the liquor then hung his head in despair. "They'll kill me."

"They will," O'Connell agreed. "If they ever get the chance, but as I said, I'll kill them for you."

"You know about the Germans, if so, then you must have seen how big they were. If they couldn't defeat those other four men, what chance have you got?"

"Size doesn't have a damn thing to do with killing.

Anyway, what do you have to lose? If I fail to kill them, you're dead. If you don't hire me, you're just as dead."

"I could go to the police."

"You could at that, and then those punks would tell them how you hired the Germans to kill them. The coppers would lock you up, and a man like you wouldn't last for long in prison."

Sid Hershel's eyes flicked toward the safe again. "You want all my money? That would put me out of business."

"Why do you still have the money at all? Didn't those hoodlums want it?"

Hershel sighed. "They're not as stupid as they look, at least, the English one isn't. They want me to sign over most of the business to them. They've already gotten the shoemaker down the street to agree to it."

"A long-term thinker our boy is, eh? Too bad for him he's running out of time."

"You'll really kill them?"

"Yes, but I'll want three-hundred apiece for killing them."

"That's more than I would pay you in a year."

"True, but I no longer work in the leather goods trade. Killing these men will be just the start."

"You're going to become a hired killer?"

"It's work more suited for a man than spending my life in this fetid place."

Sid Hershel wiped his sweaty brow with a handkerchief. "In this city, with the crime we have, you'll have no problem finding work."

Hershel paid O'Connell his money and O'Connell gave the man some advice.

"Do you have a wife, children?"

"No."

"Then find a hotel and stay there tonight."

"How will I know you've killed them?"

"I'll leave them out in the open to be found. Their deaths should make the morning paper."

As O'Connell was leaving, Hershel called to him. "You're a tanner, right?"

"You mean my name?"

"I only know you people by the jobs you do for me, and you're one of the leather tanners."

O'Connell stared at Hershel. The man had been paying him off the books, but one would think he would have bothered to learn his name. Meanwhile, his fellow workers never even spoke to him, as they considered him an outsider.

Hershel didn't know who he was, and O'Connell saw no reason to enlighten him. If the man ever talked about the killings, he'd have no true name to give anyone.

"Call me Tanner."

"That's not really your name, is it?" Hershel asked.

"It is now," O'Connell said.

Sid Hershel grabbed his coat. "I'll walk out with you, just in case those men show up."

O'Connell escorted Hershel four blocks away to a cheap hotel. Afterward, he went off into the night to kill four men.

Keane O'Connell didn't know it at the time, but he was about to spawn a legend.

5

BUSINESS TO SETTLE

WYOMING, PRESENT DAY

AFTER EVERYONE AT SPENSER'S HOUSE HAD EATEN THEIR
meal of grilled meat and salad, they sat around a picnic
table and talked. When there was a lull in the conversation,
Spenser broke the news.

"I know this was supposed to be a vacation for all of us,
but I have to work tomorrow, and I'm hoping you boys will
lend me a hand."

Tanner and Romeo perked up, as they sat straighter
and set down their beer bottles.

"If you need help, it must be serious," Tanner said.

"It's not that, but I need three people guarded while I
take care of business elsewhere. Let me explain."

Spenser went on to tell them about a former client
named Andrea Jackson. Andrea was the wife of Calvin
Jackson, who went by the nickname, Tricks. Tricks and his
two partners, who were brothers, sold heroin.

Tricks was a born liar who had Andrea believing he

was a legitimate businessman. Andrea only learned the truth when Tricks made a deal with the Feds to save himself and set up his partners, Daryl and Kevin Greene.

The Greene brothers went to prison, Andrea filed for divorce, but then, she was being threatened by a relative of the Greene brothers, Hakeem Robertson. Hakeem took Andrea and her two children hostage and promised to kill them if Tricks didn't give himself up as a trade.

Not only did Tricks not sacrifice himself, but he ran, and didn't bother to call the police. He feared that involving the police might endanger the plea agreement he'd made. Tricks was on probation for ten years, and if the authorities thought he was involved with a thug like Hakeem Robertson, he believed they might send him to jail.

Fortunately, Andrea had contacted Spenser through a mutual acquaintance after fearing that someone was stalking her. Spenser handled Hakeem, and Andrea sent the despicable Tricks out of her and her children's lives for good.

"Daryl and Kevin Greene are being paroled tomorrow. From what I know about them, they'll go straight for Tricks and kill him," Spenser said.

"What's the problem with that?" Tanner asked.

"Nothing, as far as I'm concerned," Spenser said. "But Andrea contacted me and asked me to keep him safe. She'll never let him back in her life, but he is the father of her children."

"What do you want us to do while you're saving the dirtbag?" Romeo asked.

"I want you to watch over Andrea and her children. Tricks was living where they still live now when the Greene Brothers went to jail. I think they're smart enough to get his current address, but if they aren't, then they'll head for Andrea's house."

"How old are the kids?" Tanner asked.

Spenser pressed buttons on his phone as he answered. "I'm sending you and Romeo photos of Andrea and the children."

Tanner picked up his phone and looked at the attachments on Spenser's email. Andrea Jackson was an attractive woman in her thirties with green eyes and strawberry-blonde hair. Her daughter, Jasmine, was fifteen, beautiful, and had large eyes alight with intelligence. The boy, Ethan, was ten. He wore a devilish grin in his photo.

Tanner looked up and met Romeo's eye.

Romeo nodded at him. "I'm in, Bro. It'll be like the old days."

"Not quite," Spenser said. "I'm almost certain that the Greene brothers will come for Tricks and not his family. Daryl and Kevin Greene made a lot of money selling heroin before they went to prison. I'm sure they hired someone to track Tricks down."

"Why isn't this guy Tricks on the run again?" Romeo asked.

"Andrea is sure he doesn't know that the Greene brothers were paroled early. He's gone downhill over the years. He's gambled away most of his money and lives in a trailer on land his grandfather left him. In her email, Andrea wrote that she thought he'd probably drink himself to death someday."

"How does she know so much about him if she never wants to see him again?" Tanner asked.

"Andrea and one of Tricks' female cousins are still friends. The cousin keeps Andrea informed about Tricks."

Nadya pointed at Spenser, then at Tanner. "Romeo better come back in one piece."

Romeo kissed her. "You know I can handle myself, baby."

Nadya was cradling Florentina in one arm while reaching for a baby bottle with her free hand. She looked over at Romeo, and there was worry in her gaze.

Tanner saw the look in her eyes, then spoke to Romeo. "You've had some trouble lately?"

Romeo shrugged. "There are still a lot of pirates around Indonesia. I ran across a group of them while out on our boat. They were attacking a yacht, so I lent a hand and killed four of the bastards."

"Did any of them get away?" Spenser asked.

"Yeah, but it's been a few weeks now and nothing's happened. I guess they never got a good look at my boat."

"I'm there if you need me," Tanner said.

"We'll both be there," Spenser agreed.

"Thanks, but the truth is, we're thinking of moving here to the states. Ever since Nadya's mother passed away, there's nothing keeping us in Indonesia."

"You could move to Wyoming," Spenser said.

"Nah, Spenser. Nadya and I love the boat life too much for that, but maybe we'll wind up in Florida."

LATER THAT EVENING, TANNER WENT DOWN INTO THE home's basement and made a few entries in the Book of Tanner. He then leafed through the pages, reading the exploits and observations of the men who came before him. In many ways, the book was a family album.

The basement was large. It contained a tool room, a workout room, and several gun safes. There was also a desk, and that was where Tanner sat while writing. He had recorded the activities he had performed while working with Conrad Burke, along with his association with the mysterious government official, Thomas Lawson.

He had yet to write down the exploits that occurred during his hunt for and killing of Maurice Scallato. That would take time and interlaced in the telling would be the personal details of his new relationship with Sara.

Each Tanner was free to write as much or as little about their personal lives as they pleased. The first Tanner, Keane O'Connell, had been forthcoming about the pain of losing his wife and child, along with the death of his brother. O'Connell had set the tone for what the book would be, and each subsequent Tanner had likewise shared details about their own lives.

Placing his thoughts and feelings down on paper was difficult for Tanner, but he thought it was important to do. The Book of Tanner was the only written record of the men who followed in O'Connell's footsteps.

Spenser's entries had helped Tanner understand his mentor in a way he never had before, and he deemed the book, with its wealth of experience and tactics, to be a huge advantage. Every time he wrote in it, he felt honored to do so.

Spenser came downstairs and slapped Tanner on the back. "I like Sara. I think you've finally found your match."

"She likes you too, Spenser, but I'm not sure Amy is a fan of Sara's. She seems to be keeping Sara at a distance."

"Cody, you know that Amy and Alexa became friends. The breakup was tough on Alexa."

"Amy still talks to her?"

"Once in a while."

"How is Alexa doing?"

"She's well."

Tanner nodded, and when he said nothing else, Spenser laughed.

"What's so funny?" Tanner asked.

"You are. Any other man would have wanted to know if Alexa was seeing someone, but not you. I always admired that about you. You have the ability to let things go and not dwell on them."

"Alexa is a beautiful young woman. I assume she's seeing someone."

Spenser grew serious. "It's someone you know, Cody. A man named Deke Mercer."

Tanner let out a long breath. "I thought that might happen. Alexa could do worse than Deke."

Spenser pulled out a chair and sat. "Tell me about this cousin of yours. He's the husband of Dr. Jessica White?"

"Yeah," Tanner said with a smile. "And he's something else. He's also the strongest man I've ever met."

"I'd like to meet him someday. It's good to know that you still have blood relatives, although I hope you'll always think of me as family."

"Spenser. If not for you, I'd be dead. And Romeo, Nadya, and now Florentina, they're my family too."

"Nadya always knew you and Sara would wind up together. That girl is spooky sometimes the way she can read the future."

Tanner grinned. "She was only twelve when she told Romeo that she would be his wife."

"Do you remember what he said to her?" Spenser asked with a smile.

Tanner nodded, paused, then did a perfect impersonation of Romeo.

"If I marry you, little chick, they'll lock me up and throw away the key."

Spenser laughed. "You always could mimic him well."

"You'd never know that he grew up in Texas," Tanner said.

"Romeo's a surfer dude at heart, always has been," Spenser said, and then he pointed at the book. "Have you come across anyone who might make a good Tanner Eight someday?"

Tanner thought about that. "You know, I have. There's a kid named Henry who lives in Pennsylvania. He has the heart of a lion, but he's still just a boy."

"I wonder if Keane O'Connell ever dreamed that there would still be a Tanner a hundred years after he took on the name for himself."

"He didn't," Tanner said. "That first night, that initial contract, he was just trying to find a place for himself in the world."

Spenser picked up the book, then carefully opened it to read the first few pages, pages that had been penned by Keane O'Connell.

6

I'M TANNER

CHICAGO 1917

O'CONNELL WAS HEADED TO KILL THE FOUR THUGS WHEN he saw them emerge from the alley that led to the house they'd been living in.

He had assumed they would bury the bodies of the two Germans, and perhaps they had, but given the fact that they each carried sacks or suitcases, he thought it more likely that they had decided to find a new place to flop. They must have had the spot picked out ahead of time, because they settled inside another abandoned home a half hour's walk from the first one.

At one point, the men had grown loud, and O'Connell understood that they had plans to get drunk before visiting a local whorehouse named Sally's Place. O'Connell had never been inside Sally's Place, but Davin had gone there once. Keane's younger brother had come back satisfied, but also disgusted.

"There are some beautiful women there, Keane, but

also girls, and I mean young girls. Any man that puts it to a child must be a pig."

O'Connell had counseled his brother to find himself a nice Irish girl… but Davin had never lived long enough to take that advice.

The four young thugs entered a pub and bellied up to the bar. O'Connell entered, ordered a beer, then settled himself at a small corner table. Of the four men, the Englishman was the one O'Connell deemed a threat. The man was taller and broader than his companions and O'Connell saw that the thug never relaxed his guard despite downing several drinks. Every man entering the bar was studied and evaluated mentally by the Englishman, and he had looked O'Connell's way more than once.

Seeking to put the man at ease, O'Connell left the bar first, then took up a position that would allow him to watch the pub's exit. When the men left the pub and sauntered off in the direction of Sally's Place, O'Connell headed toward the whorehouse ahead of them.

SALLY'S PLACE LOOKED LIKE ANY OTHER HOME ON THE block, except for the two men on the front porch, one of whom was sitting in a rocking chair and holding a shotgun. It was a pump-action shotgun, and O'Connell decided it would be the perfect weapon to use on his targets. At the right distance, the spread of the pellets might hit all four men if fired while they were standing close together. That would reduce the risk of the thugs returning fire.

His prey came staggering along the street as O'Connell slipped behind a row of hedges. Once at the house, the men were greeted by the guards on the porch. That was when O'Connell learned that the Englishman's name was Taylor.

Apparently, the men were regulars, but to O'Connell's surprise, they didn't enter the house. Instead, the man with the shotgun left the porch and went inside. When he returned, the man had a redheaded woman with him. She was no young skirt, and looked to be in her forties, but O'Connell thought she was a fine-looking lass. He then realized that she was Sally, the madam of the home, and not one of its offerings.

"Hello, Taylor," the woman said. "You have great timing. I just acquired a girl that you would love."

"I've always been lucky, Sally, and I have a bit of spare cash tonight."

The woman met the Englishman at the foot of the steps and they haggled in low tones. After reaching an agreement, the Englishman gave the woman a chunk of the money he had taken off the Germans he and his friends had killed. O'Connell had only caught a glimpse of the money through the hedge, but it seemed a princely sum to spend on the rental of four whores.

The man with the shotgun led the men along a dirt path that had been worn into the grass at the side of the home. It took them to the rear of the property. O'Connell followed by moving along behind the row of hedges, while staying back a good twenty feet.

At the rear of the property was another structure. It was a large shed that had been converted to living quarters. The man with the shotgun opened the door, fumbled around inside, and an electric light came on. It was a wonder to O'Connell. He was used to homes having electricity in a city like Chicago, but it seemed an extravagance to have power running to what was once no more than a shed.

A third guard came out a back door of the home, and he was not alone. There was a child with him, a girl who looked to be no more than fifteen. O'Connell was disgusted when he realized that she was to be given to the four men to abuse.

He nearly revealed himself when he saw the man escorting her slap her across the back of her head. The girl was crying and had tried to free her arm from his grip. She had long blonde hair, but it was tangled and dirty.

"She's a feisty one," Taylor said while laughing. "Don't worry, me and my mates will take the fight right out of her."

The guard holding the girl spoke in a deep baritone. "Sally said you boys could break her in, but don't mark her face."

The Brit winked at the man. "She might be a little bruised around the lips."

The guard had no sense of humor or just didn't like sick jokes, but he pointed at the Brit with a thick finger. "Don't fuck up her face, or we'll fuck up *your* face."

The Brit sighed, then reached out to grab the girl by the wrist. The girl kicked at him but missed. The Brit, Taylor, slapped the back of the girl's head the same way the guard had, only with more force. That made the girl fall to her knees, and Taylor pointed down at her.

"You could stay on your knees like that all night, you little tart, right, boys?"

The other men hooted in laughter, as the girl's escort headed back to the house.

O'Connell watched the four thugs force the girl inside the shed, and slam the door shut behind them. The man with the shotgun stared at the door for a moment, but then spun on his heels to head back toward the porch.

O'Connell made his move when the man was halfway

along the path. He had slid up behind the man by walking along the edge of the grass. After snaking an arm around to cover the guard's mouth, O'Connell slid a blade between the man's ribs. He had planned to leave the guard alive, if unconscious, but after watching the man do nothing to protect a child, O'Connell held no regard for him.

The brute struggled mightily, and O'Connell lost his balance and fell to the ground with the man, as the shotgun dropped onto the grass beside them. And still he kept stabbing away with the knife, sapping the other man's vital force with each cut. The brief struggle ended, and O'Connell stood above the dying man, only to bend over and claim the shotgun.

The girl's screams were laced amid the men's sick laughter, but both sounds ended when O'Connell kicked open the door. The girl was lying on her back on a mattress. Her dress had been torn from her torso, revealing a pair of pale freckled breasts. Three of the men were clustered together, with one down on his knees at the girl's side. The three all had their pants down to their ankles, while the Englishman stood in a corner and had just unbuttoned his britches.

The man who'd been holding the girl down released her and struggled to his feet O'Connell, with the shotgun pressed against his shoulder, fired at the three men who stood together. One man died right away. He was the man in the middle and had caught most of the pellets. The other two men fell to the floor clutching their faces, while screaming in agony.

O'Connell pumped the shotgun and fired at the Brit as the other man was bringing out a gun. Pellets shredded the Brit's chest and ripped a gash in his throat. After pumping in another shell, O'Connell reached down and helped the girl up from the mattress. She was splattered with blood and appeared shocked by the violence, but she didn't fight him and was willing to move where he guided her.

The two men thrashing on the floor received another blast as shouts came from the house. Although the men on the floor were still alive, O'Connell knew they would die in minutes from their wounds. He had fulfilled his first contract as a hired killer.

O'Connell snaked an arm around the girl's waist and lifted her up. He then kicked at the thin wood that was the back wall of the shed. The wall panel was behind a curtain. When the panel fell out, the curtain covered the opening in the wall.

O'Connell stepped outside with the shotgun leading the way. Behind the home was a stretch of trees, and O'Connell said a prayer of thanks for the bright and nearly full moon shining overhead. He moved as fast as he could, with the girl held in one arm and the shotgun in the other, until he came to the rear of a row of shops. It was after hours, and business had ended for the day.

After leaning the shotgun against a wall, O'Connell's knife made short work of a lock on a back door. He was pleased to see that he had broken into a thrift shop.

He placed the girl on her feet. She stirred from her shock enough to cover her exposed breasts with her hands, then she stared at O'Connell with eyes full of trepidation.

O'Connell grabbed a dress from a rack, deemed it to be the right size, and handed it to the girl. "Take that, lass, it should fit you."

After turning her back, the girl put the dress on, then wiped the blood splatter from her face with the remains of her old dress. She turned to stare at O'Connell again, and there was less fear in her eyes.

He sent her a grim smile. "What's your name, Lass?"

"Eloise Murphy."

"How did you wind up in that house, Eloise?"

Tears rolled down the girl's cheeks. "My father sold me to Miss Sally this morning. He needed the money to pay off a gambling debt."

O'Connell let out a sound of disgust. After finding a shirt and a pair of slacks that would fit him, he removed his bloody work clothes and changed into the new shirt and pants, while hidden from Eloise's sight by a stack of boxes.

O'Connell then picked out an overcoat, one long enough to conceal the shotgun. When he was done, he walked over and tossed money on the counter. He was an assassin, not a thief.

"Sir?" Eloise said. "Did you kill those men to save me?"

"No, lass. I killed those men because I was paid to do it, but I'd be damned if I would leave you behind to the tender mercies of Miss Sally."

Eloise moved closer and O'Connell saw that her eyes were as green as his own. O'Connell also realized that the girl was a bit older than he had guessed earlier and was likely past her sixteenth birthday.

"What's your name?" Eloise asked.

O'Connell smiled.

"I'm Tanner."

7

FRANK RECTI

O'CONNELL TOOK ELOISE TO AN ALL-NIGHT EATERY THAT catered to the staff of a hospital.

The girl was ravenous and told O'Connell that she had not eaten since the day before yesterday. He guessed they were not the first meals the child had missed. She told him that she was a month away from turning seventeen, yet she looked small for her age.

"You have any other family besides your father?"

Eloise looked stricken by his question, and O'Connell understood why.

"I won't take you back to your father."

"You promise?"

"I just did. I'm not a liar, lass."

"I don't have anyone else, Tanner."

"Then I guess you're on your own."

"Could I stay with you?"

"No, but I'll help you settle in somewhere."

Eloise yawned, then looked at O'Connell with drooping eyes. "I'm so tired."

O'Connell paid the bill and walked with Eloise to his

rooming house. The basement room where Davin had died had been cleaned and reorganized months earlier, but O'Connell knew that a pair of old army cots were among the junk scattered in the basement.

He set the cots up, and after Eloise used the toilet, O'Connell covered her with a musty blanket taken from a box of stored items.

"I'll have to wake you early so no one sees us leave."

Eloise nodded at him even as she was falling asleep. O'Connell cleaned the dust off an eastward facing window and positioned his cot so the morning sun would wake him. He fell asleep while staring over at Eloise. The girl reminded him of his first love, Bridget O'Hara, only Bridget had died of pneumonia when she was fourteen.

He drifted to sleep, his mind at ease, and his pockets full of cash.

ELOISE ROSE AT FIRST LIGHT WITHOUT COMPLAINT. O'Connell had gone through the old clothing in the basement and filled a suitcase full of clothes for Eloise. He had also come up with a disguise for her.

"Those are boy's clothes," Eloise said, while staring at the pants O'Connell was handing her.

"I know that, but if you dress like a boy I can sneak you upstairs into the bathroom where you can get properly clean."

Eloise took the clothes as she sighed. "I would love to be clean."

With her long hair tucked under a cap, Eloise made for a passable boy, and O'Connell snuck her upstairs. They had to wait inside his room, after realizing that someone was already in the communal bathroom.

The wait was a short one, and after bathing, O'Connell led Eloise back down to the basement, where she changed into a dress O'Connell had found for her. The garment was a little old-fashioned, but it fit her well and matched the shoes she wore.

"Do you have any skills, child?"

"I can sew. I can even make dresses. My grandmother taught me how when I was little."

O'Connell rubbed a hand over his chin as a thought occurred to him. They spent time walking about and watching the city awaken to a new day. That was followed by breakfast at a café that also had pastry. Eloise's appetite was as strong as the previous night, and the thin girl ate breakfast along with two pastries called olykoeks. An olykoek was a ball-shaped cake made of sweetened dough, much like a donut hole treat.

Just after ten in the morning, O'Connell escorted the girl into a dress shop he used to pass by on his way to work at Sid Hershel's tannery. O'Connell held the morning paper in one hand as he opened the dress shop door for Eloise. Its headline told of the five men who had died the night before at a house of ill repute. The four thugs, along with the bodyguard who'd had the shotgun.

O'Connell wrinkled his brow in concern when he read that the murders were being attributed to a mobster named Frank Recti.

FRANK RECTI ENTERED SID HERSHEL'S TANNERY WITH TWO other men and headed straight for the office. Hershel had been seated at his desk with a big smile on his face, as he took in the headline on the newspaper before him.

When he looked up and saw Frank Recti, the smile

turned into a worried frown. He thought he was staring up at three police officers.

"May I help you gentlemen?" Hershel asked.

"The coppers been to see you?" Recti asked. His voice was like a harsh whisper. He was thirty-five, but while still a teenager, he had survived an attacker using a garrote in the stairway of a North Side tenement. The attacker hadn't survived, and Recti had taken over his territory. The voice was notable, as was Recti's dark hair, which sat in a tangle above his head looking as if it had rarely been combed.

"You aren't the police?" Hershel asked.

"I'm Frank Recti. You've heard of me, yes?"

Hershel knew the name, as well as Recti's reputation.

"Four pieces of vermin were gunned down last night. These were men trying to invade a part of my territory. Luckily for me, I have an alibi, but I hear these men were giving you trouble. I was also told that you were seen talking to the Heinz brothers."

Sid Hershel opened his mouth, but nothing came out. He swallowed, tried again, and tentative words left his lips.

"The Heinz brothers are dead."

"What do you mean?"

"The Englishman and his men killed them."

"So, who killed the Englishman?"

"An Irishman. He calls himself Tanner."

Frank Recti leaned over the desk and gave Hershel a skeptical look. "One man killed those men at the brothel?"

"Yes."

"How do you know him?"

"He worked here for a short time."

"This Tanner, what's his first name?"

"I don't know. These men come and go, but he calls himself Tanner now."

Frank Recti reached into a pocket and took out twenty

dollars. "Tell your people out there that I'll give two sawbucks to whoever can tell me where this man Tanner lives."

Hershel looked over at the money and silently cursed himself for not keeping records.

Within minutes, one of the other workers claimed the reward, which was more than the man made in a week. The man said that he didn't know exactly where the Irishman lived, but he often saw him walking home past his own residence. If Recti's men kept watch in the area, they had a good chance of spotting Tanner.

Recti then told Hershel to give him twenty-five dollars. Hershel handed over the money, and Recti smiled at him.

"There will be a man dropping by every week from now on. You'll give him twenty-five dollars and you won't have any more problems here, understand?"

"Yes, sir."

"I'll also be taking your man with me, so he can point out this guy Tanner. You got a problem with that?"

"No, sir. Whatever you say, sir."

Sid Hershel watched the corners of Frank Recti's lips rise into a sick little smile. He could tell the man enjoyed the fear he had induced in him.

Recti spun on his heels and headed for the door. "Let's go find this Tanner, boys."

~

AN HOUR AFTER ENTERING THE DRESS SHOP, ELOISE HAD A job as a seamstress that came with a cot in a back room. The woman who owned the shop had been desperate to hire someone for weeks, after her daughter eloped and ran off to the west coast.

O'Connell had claimed to be Eloise's father and a

Merchant Marine who had just lost his wife. The owner of the shop told him that she would keep an eye on Eloise and see that she behaved like a proper young lady.

When it was time to part ways, Eloise walked outside with O'Connell and smiled up at him.

"Thank you, Tanner. I think I'll like it here."

"The lady seems a decent sort."

"Are you really a sailor?"

"No, lass. I spewed vomit every day on the trip over here from Ireland."

Eloise laughed, then lunged at O'Connell to embrace him in a fierce hug. "Thank you for saving me last night," she whispered.

"It was my pleasure, Eloise. Men like that aren't fit to live."

"They were no different than my father," Eloise said, and O'Connell understood that life had not been kind to Eloise.

As the hug ended, Eloise made a request. "Please come see me. Not right away, but please do come."

O'Connell nodded. "I'll pop in on you someday."

He reached into a pocket, removed a roll of bills, and peeled off a number of them. Eloise took the offered money with wide eyes. She had never seen so much cash in her life.

"Now, don't you go spending that money on silly trinkets and such. That money is to be saved for a rainy day."

"I understand, Tanner, and thank you."

Tanner sighed as he looked at the girl standing before him. She really did remind him of his childhood sweetheart.

"Goodbye, Eloise, and may Saint Mary herself protect you."

O'Connell watched Eloise return to the shop. He then strode off toward his rooming house. He was going to gather his things and find a decent apartment. Had he known about the two men waiting to pounce on him, he might have left his scant belongings behind.

8

OLD DOG, OLD TRICKS

WYOMING, PRESENT DAY

Sara kissed Tanner goodbye, as Amy and Nadya did the same with their men, then she told Tanner to be careful.

"I'm always careful."

"No, you're not. It's just that your opponents die before they can do you much harm."

Tanner kissed her again, a quick one. "Be good while I'm gone."

"When have you ever known me to be good?"

"Never," Tanner said, "But try to fake it."

Romeo released Nadya, then kissed his daughter. Little Florentina cried when her daddy released her, but soon found comfort in her mother's arms.

"I'm hoping we'll be back sometime tonight," Spenser said. "The Greene brothers aren't the patient type. If they go after Tricks, they'll do it right away."

AFTER THE MEN LEFT, THE WOMEN HEADED BACK INSIDE THE house and settled in the living room. Sara sent Amy a smile, which was returned, but it seemed to Sara that the smile lacked any real warmth. When Nadya got up with Florentina to head to the kitchen for a baby bottle, Sara found herself alone with Amy. The two women stared at each other until Sara broke the silence.

"I understand you and Alexa are friends?"

"Yes."

"I hope she's doing well."

"She is, and she's spoken about you."

"I liked Alexa," Sara said.

"But you liked Cody more, didn't you?"

Sara heard the tone of disapproval in Amy's voice.

"Amy, I don't know what Alexa might have told you, but nothing happened between Tanner and I until after Alexa left him."

"But you insinuated yourself into his life before that, didn't you?"

"I sought Tanner out, yes, but that was a business matter. At the time, I had no interest in him."

"Whatever you say, Sara."

Amy stood and walked out of the room. Sara slumped back on the sofa. If the tension between her and Amy remained, it was going to be a less than pleasurable vacation.

SPENSER REACHED THE PROPERTY WHERE CALVIN "Tricks" Jackson lived and explored it on foot, while keeping his hand near his gun. The property was just shy of fourteen acres, and so it took him over an hour to roam the area.

Out behind the trailer, he came upon a spot where someone had attempted to start a garden. There was a hole there, along with an abandoned shovel and pickaxe. The soil was rocky, too rocky for farming, and the land was bordered on three sides by government property. Wyoming was mostly government-owned land, since the Federal and State Governments controlled over fifty-percent of Wyoming.

When Spenser was certain that no one else was around, he headed for Tricks' home, which was a dilapidated double-wide trailer. There was an old car parked near a shed and a dirt bike sat next to the trailer's front steps.

Spenser crept closer and could hear voices inside. One of them sounded like Tricks, but the other voice was young and female. Spenser waited by the shed. Ten minutes later, a teenage girl stepped outside and hurried to get on her dirt bike. There was a piece of foil in her hand that likely contained drugs, while Tricks had a whisky bottle tucked under his arm.

Tricks was still zipping himself up, and Spenser wondered if the girl had traded sex for drugs. The thought sickened him. It was bad enough that the girl was barely of age, but she must have been desperate for a fix to touch a toad like Tricks.

Tricks Jackson was forty-three, but looked older, and wore his brown hair long. He had gone to jail twice as a young man, and he was a scumbag.

Andrea Jackson was refined, college educated, and beautiful. Spenser had always wondered how Andrea could have been fooled by a mutt like Tricks. Although, to be fair, Tricks had been looking better when Andrea became involved with him. The years of alcohol abuse had aged the man and lined his face. Tricks sat on the steps, gulped down some whisky, then watched the girl ride off. It caused him to look away from where Spenser was standing.

Spenser tossed a pebble over the trailer. The sound of the stone landing made Tricks turn his head even more. When Tricks decided that the sound had been made by an unseen animal, he turned back around and found Spenser staring at him.

Tricks dropped the bottle, then tried to scramble inside the trailer on his hands and knees. Spenser grabbed a handful of greasy hair and yanked Tricks backwards, making the man fall to the ground.

"I see you remember me," Spenser said.

"A dude with an eyepatch who threatened to kill me? Fuck yeah, I remember you. But I swear man, I haven't talked to Andrea in years."

"I know, but you've got trouble headed your way. Andrea asked me to save your sorry butt."

Tricks sat up, a big smile on his face. The smile was still a good one, full of gleaming white teeth.

"If Andrea is worried about me, that must mean she wants me back."

"I told you I would kill you if you ever went near Andrea again. I still mean that."

Tricks' smile widened. "You can't stop true love, my man."

"Daryl and Kevin Greene are headed your way," Spenser said, and was pleased to see the smile on Tricks' face vanish.

∾

Andrea Jackson's house was in a small town that had seen better days. Two years earlier, the local Big-Box store closed, taking over two-hundred jobs along with it. The resulting unemployment hurt other businesses in the community. With less people working and shopping, less fuel was needed for commuters, and the area's gas stations saw a huge drop in business. The same was true for the local auto repair shops, as seldom used vehicles needed less maintenance.

Andrea was doing well personally, because she ran an online business, but the small charming town she wanted to raise her children in was disappearing, along with its prosperity.

Tanner stepped out of his rental and looked about. Andrea's home was of average size but had a decent front yard and half an acre of grass in the rear. The backyard was bordered by trees that stretched back toward the highway. The neighborhood was quiet, and many of the other lawns looked unkempt.

In the distance loomed the roof of the building that had once employed many in the small town. Solar panels were set in rows above the tar-covered surface, and the panels gleamed like polished mirrors.

Andrea Jackson stepped out onto her front porch and sent Tanner a cautious smile, but her eyes roamed over Romeo and she sent him a genuine grin. She was dressed in jeans and a white long-sleeve T-Shirt, and she met them at the foot of her porch steps.

After introductions, Andrea spoke. "Spenser called and explained why you're here. But do you really think we're at risk?"

Romeo waved that off. "We're like insurance in case Spenser is wrong about the Greene brothers, but if

Spenser really thought you were in danger, we would be moving you to another location."

Andrea smiled at Romeo. "Still, you're very brave to do this."

"What have you told the children?" Tanner asked.

"They know the truth, well, part of it. Jasmine was ten when we were threatened, and while Ethan was only five, they both remember that their father abandoned them to die. I never want to lay eyes on that bastard again, but if I hadn't contacted Spenser, it would have been like killing Calvin myself, and I couldn't do that."

"I'm curious," Romeo said. "Why didn't you call the cops?"

Andrea leaned forward and spoke in a low voice. "They wouldn't protect Calvin... not the way Spenser will."

The children came out onto the porch. When Jasmine saw Tanner, her mouth formed an O and she blushed. Ethan ran down the stairs and looked up at them. He wore the same devilish grin Tanner had seen in the picture Spenser had sent him.

"You guys have guns, right? Can I see them?"

"Afraid not, little dude," Romeo said.

The boy frowned, then walked back up the steps and into the house. They followed him inside, and as Tanner was introduced to her, Jasmine giggled nervously.

"It's nice to meet you, Mr. Tanner."

"No mister, just call me Tanner."

"Okay," Jasmine said breathlessly.

Ethan merely sent them a wave when his mother introduced him. "I'm going to play my Xbox," the boy said.

Andrea called after him. "Keep the volume down, and lunch is in an hour."

Romeo and Tanner asked to be given a tour of the home, so that they could check for unlocked windows and judge any angles of fire they might need. They'd been told by Spenser that the house had one staircase that led up to a second floor. Three bedrooms and a master bath made up that floor, along with a small bathroom in the hall.

The ground floor opened onto a living room to the left of the staircase, and beyond the living room was a hallway. A small home office and a powder room sat off the hall, which ended at a large kitchen.

As Andrea was leading them toward the hall, Ethan came running down the stairs with a frightened look on his face.

"Men! There are two men with guns in my room and they tried to grab me."

Tanner's gun was in his hand so fast it was as if he had conjured it into existence. "Romeo?"

"Go, Bro, I got them."

Tanner flew up the stairs, his gun at the ready, as behind him, Romeo herded the family out of the home to safety.

9

ONE TOUGH MICK

CHICAGO 1917

KEANE O'CONNELL WAS RELIEVED TO SEE THAT THERE were no police cars parked in front of his rooming house.

He'd known that there was an outside chance the authorities would tie the dead Brit to Sid Hershel. If that had happened, Hershel would have given him up in a flash.

His plans were to stay at a hotel until he found an apartment. Once he was settled, he'd haunt the waterfront taverns and learn who the men were that ran the city's underbelly. They would be the men that would hire him to kill. Killing had never bothered O'Connell, and he doubted it ever would. He wasn't a butcher and had no desire to murder for no reason. But he was good at killing, was as tough as they came, and found the work interesting when the target was difficult or well protected. If mobsters wanted to pay him to kill other mobsters, he would gladly take their money.

As O'Connell approached his rooming house, a man walked by him. He was an older man, and the eyeglasses he wore were huge. O'Connell had seen other men wearing such eyewear, and thought the trend was a strange one. It would be bad enough to need eyeglasses, but why attract attention to yourself by wearing such huge frames?

As he turned his head to watch the man walk by, he spotted the men staring at him. There were two of them. O'Connell walked past his rooming house and made a right at the next corner. The men followed.

They weren't coppers. O'Connell was sure of that, because the police would have just scooped him up and taken him in for questioning.

O'Connell went up the steps of another apartment house. Once inside the building, he moved up the stairs swiftly as if he were going home. When he glanced back, he found that the men were coming up behind him. They wanted to grab him, not kill him, otherwise they would be shooting.

When one of them came up beside him on the third floor, the man took out a gun and pointed it at him.

"You're Tanner?" the man asked.

O'Connell didn't answer, because he had just realized that a third man was involved. It was a face he knew from Sid Hershel's tannery. Somehow, the man had been used to track him down.

The man with the gun saw where he was looking. He called down to the man standing on the landing.

"You did your job, now scram."

The tannery worker tipped his hat and scurried away down the stairs. O'Connell studied the two men that remained. Both men wore suits that looked expensive, while the man with the gun wore a white pair of spats. Spats, which was short for spatter guards, were seldom worn in Chicago. Most of the streets were paved, and there was little risk of stepping in mud.

"I asked you a question," the man said.

"I'm Tanner. Who are you?" O'Connell asked.

"Frank Recti wants to see you."

O'Connell knew Recti's name from the morning paper. The man was being blamed for the killing of the four men O'Connell had murdered. Meeting Frank Recti at gunpoint did not strike O'Connell as a good idea.

The other man laughed. He held no gun, but he was big and tough-looking. "Don't try running, bud, Al there will just shoot you in the leg."

O'Connell nodded his understanding and the two men flanked him. The man with the gun held on to O'Connell's arm with a loose grip as the other man did the same with the other arm. The gun was still out but hidden beneath the man's jacket.

When they reached the landing that led down to the lobby, O'Connell shook his arms free and backed up, as if he were going to turn and race up the stairs.

As the two men turned, placing their backs to the staircase, O'Connell reached out, grabbed them by their ties, then leapt up and planted his feet against their stomachs.

Shock lit the faces of both men as they fell backwards down the staircase with O'Connell riding on them as if they were a pair of skis.

Loud grunts came from both men as their backs slammed against the steps. That was followed by a shout of pain as the man wearing the spats broke a bone in his wrist. The gun he'd been holding in his other hand tumbled away, and the weapon clunked along on the wooden boards.

O'Connell released his own grunt as they hit bottom,

for he had fallen backwards upon losing his grip on the men's ties.

His abductors moaned before him from their various aches and wounds, with one man, the huge man, developing an egg-sized lump on the top of his forehead. After grabbing up the weapon Spats had dropped, O'Connell searched the man with the lump and took his gun as well.

A doorway opened from somewhere above, and a woman's voice yelled down to them. "You children stop playing on those stairs!"

The door slammed shut, and O'Connell smiled down at the two men. "Let's go see this Frank Recti."

FRANK RECTI WAS SEATED IN THE BACK SEAT OF A NEW Model T. The vehicle was parked behind a fence which surrounded a construction site where an office building was going up.

Spats was driving, while the other man was seated beside him in a passenger seat that faced the rear, where O'Connell held their guns pointed at them below the level of the window. Spats' car was an electric model, a Detroit Electric. O'Connell was surprised by how quiet the machine was.

As they drove through a gate and behind the fence, O'Connell instructed Spats to pull up beside Recti's car. Once they were parked, O'Connell shoved open the door, knocking Spats to the ground, to then point his weapon at Frank Recti. He had seen a picture of the man in the morning paper and wondered if it had been taken after a windstorm. But no, apparently, Frank Recti's hair always looked that wild.

"You and your driver get out of the car."

"Your name is Tanner?" Recti asked, in his hoarse voice.

"Out of the car, or I start shooting."

Recti let loose a long sigh, then stepped from the car while instructing his driver to do the same. When the driver's hand drifted toward the holstered gun beneath his jacket, it was Recti who told him to relax.

"Tanner just wants to talk, otherwise I'd be dead by now."

"Why did you want to see me?"

"You killed four men by yourself. I wanted to know if that was luck or skill. Now I know it was skill."

"The papers wrote that the police were blaming you for the murders. Were you planning to hand me over to the police?"

"I'd sooner shoot myself than help the coppers. Besides, I had an alibi for last night."

O'Connell lowered the gun he was still holding. "Now that you know I can handle myself, what now?"

"I can use a man like you, only thing is, you're a damn Mick, so I can't make you a part of my gang. We're all Italians."

"I wouldn't join anyway, but if you ever need someone killed, I'm handy to have around."

Recti gestured about at his men. "They'll kill anyone I want dead."

"If they don't get killed first," O'Connell said.

Recti laughed. "Here's what we'll do, come by my office sometime and we'll talk. It's Recti Construction, down on State Street, near Grand Avenue."

O'Connell climbed into Spat's electric car. "I'll leave this car on State Street, so you can find it."

"And what about my men's weapons?" Recti asked.

"I'll keep those," O'Connell said. "But if your men come after me again I'll give them back their bullets."

"You're one tough Mick, Tanner," Recti said.

"Tough enough," O'Connell agreed. He drove back through the gate and was gone.

10

BUSTED BY THE LAW

KEANE O'CONNELL BEGAN WORKING FOR FRANK RECTI, but under his own terms.

The terms were simple. If he were offered a contract he didn't want to take, he could refuse it without any consequences. However, if he agreed to take a contract, he was on his own and Recti's people stayed out of it. Payment was always up front, and with O'Connell as his secret weapon, Frank Recti's fortunes rose in the circles of Chicago's organized crime.

The job of assassin left O'Connell with plenty of free time. He filled it by reading, and, in particular, by studying history, a subject that had always fascinated him. His adopted country, although young, had a vibrant past, and O'Connell thought the American West was intriguing.

He found it easy to imagine himself as an old west gunslinger, and took a train trip west to Arizona, where he traveled about as a tourist visiting famous sites. In Tombstone, Arizona, he came across an old man who had witnessed the final moments of the shootout at the O.K. Corral.

From the old man, O'Connell learned that there had been further violence between the Earps and the group of outlaws called The Cowboys. Virgil Earp was ambushed and maimed in a murder attempt, while Morgan Earp was murdered.

O'Connell learned a lesson by studying the events at the O.K. Corral. Never leave an enemy alive. If you believe a man has reason to harm you, then kill him. It was a lesson that would become a tenet of each future Tanner's training.

~

FRANK RECTI AND HIS MEN KNEW O'CONNELL BY THE name of Tanner, but O'Connell was in America under his own name and not an alias. As himself, O'Connell obeyed all the rules. He rented a secluded home in an area which would one day be annexed by landfill and become Montrose Beach.

The company of women was an infrequent pleasure, and O'Connell's sex life mainly consisted of trysts with a librarian whose husband was a career military man. O'Connell's late wife had meant the world to him, and no other woman ever made him feel the way she had. Given his illegal profession, he doubted he would ever be close to anyone, much less marry again.

He was only thirty-three, and yet, there were days he felt like an old man inside. He missed Ireland, he missed his brother, and he still ached for the touch of his late wife. Often, upon seeing a young boy, he would have to fight back tears while thinking of his dead son. While it was true the child had survived outside the womb for only a few precious days, O'Connell had loved him fiercely.

~

O'CONNELL TRAVELED TO WASHINGTON D.C. IN THE spring of 1918. The history buff had enjoyed a wonderful time exploring the city and had watched construction take place on the Lincoln Memorial. He planned to return to Washington a few years later, when the monument was scheduled to be completed.

Prior to taking the trip, O'Connell had killed three men for Frank Recti. The men were from a rival gang that had intruded into Recti's territory. Their deaths were a lesson to any others who might attempt to do the same.

O'Connell was always watchful of retribution by friends of the men he killed, but as Tanner, he was essentially a nonentity among the mob of Chicago. While there was no shortage of killers, the others all belonged to gangs. Tanner had worked solely for Recti, but he was not a member of the Black Hand, the criminal organization with which Recti was affiliated.

The Black Hand was dying anyway, as a new group, the Chicago Outfit began gaining in dominance. As Tanner, O'Connell had begun to reach out to members of the Chicago Outfit, and let it be known that he was a gun for hire.

~

WHEN HE RETURNED FROM A SWIM ONE DAY AND SAW THE police on his doorstep, O'Connell let the gun he had hidden behind his back slip into the grass. A smart man didn't fight coppers with guns. A smart man fought the police with lawyers.

One cop was older than him, while the other was younger, and it was the older cop who spoke.

"Keane O'Connell?"

"Yes?"

The cop handed him a slip of paper.

"What's this?" O'Connell asked.

"That's a notice from a judge that you're to be at the induction center on Grant Street within the next three days. You've been drafted, O'Connell. Haven't you been reading your mail?"

In truth, he hadn't, and it had piled up while he was on his trip to Washington.

"I've been away on holiday. Besides, my application for citizenship hasn't been approved yet."

"That doesn't matter."

"Are you saying that I have to join the army?"

The cop smiled. "You're already in the army, but if you don't show up for your induction, we'll be back to take you to jail."

The cops walked over to their vehicle and drove off.

O'Connell went inside and found two letters from the army. Yes, he had been drafted, and he realized that there was a good chance that he'd be shipped off to Europe to fight in what was being called the Great War.

O'Connell considered packing up and going away, but that would mean leaving Chicago, and Chicago had become his home.

Two months later, Private Keane O'Connell was on the Western Front in France.

11

STONE COLD

AFTER GETTING FLORENTINA TO SLEEP, NADYA CAME downstairs holding a baby monitor receiver and found Sara and Amy sitting apart in the living room. Sara was reading a book, while Amy was playing a game on the computer.

"I want to watch a movie," Nadya said. "It's that new one with Drake Diamond."

At the mention of the name, Drake Diamond, both Sara and Amy stopped what they were doing.

"There's a new Drake Diamond movie?" Sara asked.

Nadya grinned. "There is, and he plays a male stripper in it."

"Oh my God," Amy said, as Sara tossed her eReader aside, the book forgotten. She settled on Nadya's left, as Amy sat on Nadya's right.

"You're a Drake Diamond fan too, Amy?" Sara asked.

"Stalker might be more accurate. I once sat in front of a movie theater all night to see a sneak preview of one of his movies."

"So did I," Sara said. "It was Roman Gladiator."

Amy nodded. "That's the one, and when he did that nude scene I almost fainted."

"I still watch that sometimes," Sara said. "And I own the movie."

"I own every Drake Diamond movie," Amy said, while laughing.

Sara smiled at her, and the earlier tension they'd felt evaporated under the heat of mutual interest.

TRICKS PROTESTED AS SPENSER DRAGGED HIM ALONG BY HIS hair to the spot at the rear of the trailer, where a shovel and pick had been discarded.

After tripping him to the ground, Spenser pointed at Tricks. "Understand something. You're not running away this time. This time you're going to face the consequences."

"They want to kill me, man. I can't believe they only got five years."

"They were released early because the prisons are overcrowded, but that's what happens when a legal system decides to dispense soft cots instead of justice."

Tricks stood, and Spenser could tell by his body language that he was thinking of making a run for his car.

"If you try to run, I'll shoot you in the leg."

"That could kill me."

"Accidents happen."

Tricks looked down at the shovel. "Why did you drag me out here?"

"I want you to dig two graves."

Tricks shook his head. "I tried digging back here. I was going to grow a few plants, you know, just some weed for personal use, but there's too many rocks."

"We'll still need somewhere to bury the Greene brothers."

"Let me run. They won't find me. I'll hide in Denver. I got a cousin there."

"Listen, Tricks, I'm here to help you. If the Greene brothers try to kill you, I'll stop them."

"How?"

"That depends. I'll give the trailer a good looking over. Maybe I'll come up with a plan."

The old trailer was a pigsty. Spenser had given it a quick check for other occupants before dragging Tricks off to dig. After returning to it, he gazed about while thinking strategically.

Despite the filth and discarded liquor bottles, Tricks had a new flat screen TV that must have cost over a grand. A large mirror was suspended above the bed, and on the side table was a rolled dollar bill and traces of what Spenser took to be cocaine, but there was nowhere to take cover while opening fire.

Spenser decided that any action should take place outside. That was when he remembered a hill he had passed. The area must have flooded at some point, causing a mudslide. The water left a pile of small boulders in its wake at the base of the hill.

He walked out with Tricks to the area and gestured around. "This is still your land, right?"

"Yeah, my great-grandfather Calvin left it to me in his will. I was named after him. The guy lived to be ninety-eight, do you believe that?"

"If those rocks were cleared away from that depression in the earth, we'd have a natural grave to place the bodies in," Spenser said.

Tricks had been taking gulps of bourbon as Spenser spoke, and appeared disheartened. Spenser wondered if

Tricks was sickened by the thought of having to kill men he had at one time considered friends. But no, the weasel was just upset by the prospect of having to perform physical labor.

"Move all those damn rocks? That could take us hours, and some of them look heavy as shit."

"Not us, just you. While you're moving the rocks, I'll be keeping an eye out for the Greene brothers."

"Why do I have to do all the work?"

"Because I said so, and it's your ass we're saving."

"Let me get some gloves first. I have a pair in my car. I'll be right back."

"Nice try, now start moving those rocks."

Tricks looked down at the rocks then back up at Spenser. "You're just going to shoot two men and dump them in a hole?"

"If they force my hand by trying to kill you, yes."

Tricks looked Spenser over, as if seeing him, really seeing him for the first time. "You're one badass dude."

"Remember that. Now get to work."

With a sigh, Tricks bent down and grabbed the first of many stones.

TANNER PLACED HIS BACK AGAINST THE WALL AND AIMED upward after reaching the landing on Andrea Jackson's stairway. Below him, Romeo was rushing Andrea and her children outside, where he would place them in Tanner's rental and be ready to drive them away to safety.

Once the sounds of their departure from the house faded, Tanner listened for other sounds. The boy, Ethan, had said that two men with guns were in the house. It was not a new house, and so the floorboards creaked. And yet,

Tanner heard no sounds coming from upstairs, nor saw any shadows moving.

He ran up three steps, paused, and listened again. Nothing. There was only the quiet steady hiss of the central air unit as it sent cool air throughout the house.

Tanner raised the barrel of his gun above the level of the stairs on the left. If anyone were lying in wait and looking for something to shoot at, he had just grabbed their attention. While his opponents' eyes were drawn to the left, Tanner shot his head up and snuck a quick glance. He saw nothing but two open doorways leading into separate rooms. Even from the brief view he had, he could see that one room was a girl's, while the other belonged to the boy.

Again, there was no sound of movement. Tanner decided that the men must be hiding and waiting for him to come to them. He would do so, and then he would kill them. Once he was at the top of the stairs, Tanner moved toward the room belonging to the boy. That was where Ethan reported seeing the two men.

A thought kept nagging at Tanner. He was wondering why the men would break into a home and then not attempt to take Andrea and her children hostage. If they were looking for Andrea's ex-husband, they would have harmed her or the children until they talked and told them what they wanted to know.

Strangers on the second floor of a home in the daytime sounded more like a pair of teenage druggies acting as second-story men, while searching for electronics or jewelry to sell.

The only thing was, once discovered, teenagers would have scrambled back out the window they came in through without shutting it behind them, and all the windows appeared to be closed.

Tanner was about to continue his search when he heard someone enter the home from downstairs. Then, Romeo called to him.

"Yo, Cody. Chill, man; it's a false alarm. The kid was messing with us."

Tanner lowered his weapon, then placed it back in its holster, as he went down the stairs, to where Romeo stood alone in the hallway.

"The kid was playing a game?"

"Yeah, funny, hmm?"

Andrea joined them inside. Jasmine was staring at Tanner with a smile on her face, as Andrea dragged Ethan along by the arm. If the boy was sorry for his prank it didn't show, as a smirk was on his lips.

"Apologize to Tanner and Romeo," Andrea told her son.

"Why? I was just testing them," Ethan said.

Tanner leaned down to stare Ethan in the eye. Ethan's cocky smile vanished. He tried to maintain eye contact but couldn't bear the fierceness emanating from Tanner's intense gaze. A soft whine escaped, as the boy's knees weakened, and after gripping his mother's hand, Ethan moved behind her.

"I'll be good," he whispered.

Standing beside Ethan, his sister giggled, while Andrea gave Tanner a worried look.

"That's some set of eyes you have there, Tanner," Andrea said.

Tanner ignored her and headed toward the kitchen. "Let's check all the windows and doors, Romeo."

"Right, bro," Romeo said, and after wagging his finger at Ethan, he followed Tanner.

THE GREAT WAR

THE WESTERN FRONT, AUGUST 1918

WHILE IN THE ARMY, KEANE O'CONNELL MET THE FIRST Englishman he ever had any use for.

That man was John Stone, and Stone was a sniper who trained other snipers. Thanks to Stone's instruction, O'Connell discovered that he was just as adept at killing from a distance as he was at killing up close.

Being a sniper also gave him the opportunity to work alone, which was more suited to his nature. He could have worked with a partner, as most of the other men did. But O'Connell worked best when alone, and the officers respected his abilities. He also received a promotion to Corporal.

Along with the sniper training came the art of camouflage, and O'Connell became a master at it. Being a sniper wasn't all about killing. A camouflaged soldier could also work as a scout and determine the enemy's troop movements and artillery placements.

Keane O'Connell was so bold that he had taken to infiltrating enemy trenches and killing the men within them while they slept. He would also take officers prisoner when possible, and much intelligence was gained by questioning the men under duress.

As fearless as O'Connell was, there was one in his company who was braver, or perhaps he was just foolhardier. His name was Michael Waller, a farm boy from the Midwest.

Waller was as tall as O'Connell but had lied about his age to join the army. In truth, Michael Waller was only sixteen, but the intrepid boy ached to have a life of adventure, and what better place to begin such a life than to fight in what was being called The Great War.

Despite his age, Waller was a deadly soldier. Like O'Connell, the boy routinely snuck across enemy lines. He once stayed there for an entire day while dressed in the uniform of a German soldier. During that day, Michael Waller had killed six men. For proof, he had taken the men's dog tags. He was praised for his valor, but several men criticized him for removing the dog tags.

"How'd you like to be lying dead in a trench, boy, with no way for the officers to inform the folks back home?" asked one soldier.

From that point on, Michael Waller left the dead wearing their dog tags.

~

REGARDLESS OF THEIR AGE DIFFERENCE, O'CONNELL AND Waller became friends, and O'Connell taught the boy all he knew about camouflage.

Despite his interest in learning the skill, Waller wasn't accepted into the sniper program because the Englishmen

John Stone thought the boy lacked patience. O'Connell had agreed. An impatient sniper was a dead sniper. Once the enemy knew your position, all hell was sent your way, including artillery shelling.

O'Connell saw in Waller a quality that he'd recognized in himself. It was a stoic nature that allowed him to think and remain calm in situations where most men panicked or froze up. During the numerous gas attacks, when the men needed to don their masks, O'Connell saw grown men whimper as their faces wore expressions of terror.

He simply placed his mask on and waited for the wind to disperse the mustard gas. If his mask was defective, or if tendrils of the gas were to reach him before he could secure it over his head, then he would suffer the effects, such as painful blisters, possibly followed by a lingering death.

Being terrified and letting your imagination run away wouldn't change those outcomes. Panic might even make things worse. Life was what it was, and you had to deal with it as best as you could.

During one such attack of gas, O'Connell and Waller found themselves in the pit of a trench with five other soldiers.

Most of the men were young, although not as young as Waller. Perhaps it was inexperience, perhaps temperament, but all five of the other men were in various stages of distress from the fear they were experiencing over their terror of the gas. O'Connell looked over and saw Waller staring at him with a calm expression. Then, the boy's eyes crinkled, and O'Connell could tell he was smiling beneath the mask. Waller gestured at O'Connell, and then back at himself.

O'Connell nodded once in understanding. The boy was telling O'Connell that they were the same. They went through life, not unafraid, but unbowed, by either circumstance or the hobgoblins of fear. It was the quality that made them both exceptional soldiers. In O'Connell's case, it had also aided him in becoming a skilled assassin.

WALLER COULD READ, BUT NOT AT A LEVEL O'CONNELL deemed acceptable. He took it upon himself to school the inquisitive boy in history while also improving his literacy skills. Waller couldn't get enough. In fact, he seemed to have a knack for learning other languages as well.

Waller picked up French with ease, and taught O'Connell enough of it to get by when they had a three-day leave in Paris.

A sixteen-year-old virgin, Waller had spent his last day on leave with a girl he'd met at an outdoor café. Her parents were away, and they had the house to themselves.

He was still wearing a silly grin a week later.

O'CONNELL RETURNED AT DAYBREAK FROM A SUCCESSFUL scouting mission to discover that no one had seen Waller in two days. After reporting in and delivering the intelligence he'd gathered, O'Connell was expected to rest up for his next mission. Instead, he refilled his canteen and ammo pack, cleaned his rifle, and went out to search for Waller.

A heavy rain had fallen the previous day and the sky was still full of clouds. O'Connell made good use of the mud and slathered himself with it, to blend in with the drab landscape around him.

Two hours later he was well into enemy territory when he heard cries of pain coming from the fire-damaged remains of a French farmhouse. It was Michael Waller, and he was being tortured. The three soldiers tormenting the boy were Hungarians. One of them was an officer.

O'Connell raised his rifle, but then lowered it. The booming of the 1903 Springfield rifle might bring others on the run. O'Connell concealed his rifle in the branches of a tree, then headed toward the farmhouse while unsheathing his knife.

He came up behind the men undetected and slit the throat of the officer, then was aided by chance when the man's spurting blood blinded one of the other soldiers. The third man was reaching for the gun on his hip when O'Connell shoved the dying officer at him, making the soldier lose his balance. With no time for finesse, O'Connell slashed away with his knife like an animal raking at prey. When he was done, the officer was dead, while the two soldiers were bleeding from numerous wounds. They lay on the floor moaning in agony.

Their moans mixed with those of Michael Waller's cries of pain. Waller had been hung by bound wrists from a roof beam and beaten severely. There was also a gash in his side that dripped blood. It had likely been caused by a bayonet. The boy's eyes were both swollen shut, and so O'Connell wasn't certain he could see. However, he could hear, and when O'Connell spoke to him, a smile crept across Waller's puffy lips.

"Can you walk, lad?" O'Connell asked, and received a nod.

After finishing off the two wounded soldiers, O'Connell led Waller to the tree where he'd left his rifle. When he climbed up to retrieve his weapon, O'Connell spied four more men headed toward them.

There was no way the men would miss them, and if

they hid, the men would soon come upon the dead inside the damaged farmhouse.

It was foolhardy to use the rifle, as its sound was distinct and could bring others running, but O'Connell weighed the risk and decided to fire. The four men died one after the other as O'Connell fired and worked the bolt on his weapon. Afterward, he dropped to the ground, got Waller to his feet, and spoke with urgency.

"We need to move fast."

"I can barely see, Keane," Waller said.

"Then take my hand."

They ran at a jog, occasionally seeing the enemy, but only at a distance. The two hours spent crisscrossing the landscape while searching for Waller was far more time than they would need to get back into their own territory. Nonetheless, the enemy was active, and they had to hide several times to avoid capture.

O'Connell smiled when he saw signs that they were nearly back across the line, but he screamed in pain as a bullet struck him in the left leg. He toppled to the ground, with Waller following him there. The pain of his wound had brought tears to O'Connell's eyes, but he had maintained his grip on his rifle.

The soldier who'd shot him must have thought he'd killed him, because the fool was running toward them and shouting in German.

"Keane?" Waller whispered, as he stayed still.

"I'm alive," O'Connell said, his words twisted by agony.

O'Connell tried to push aside the pain, but the pain pushed back, and he found that he could barely hold on to his rifle. After bracing himself again, he swiped at the tears blurring his vision, then took aim. The German's head erupted in a mist of red, but there were other uniformed figures coming closer.

"Where's your injury, Keane?" Waller asked.

"My left leg."

When O'Connell tried to stand, he found that he couldn't, then felt himself being lifted by Waller and draped over his shoulders in a fireman's carry.

"Tell me which direction to run," Waller said. The words were squeezed out between teeth clenched in agony. O'Connell was amazed at the boy's stamina.

"To the right, Michael. I see a group of our men there."

Waller ran for all he was worth, but it was slow and jerky due to O'Connell's weight, the sucking mud, and his own injuries.

Waller collapsed just yards shy of a trench. When O'Connell looked at him, he saw that the boy had reached his limit and passed out. O'Connell dragged himself and the boy into the trench as his comrades traded shots with the enemy soldiers who'd been on their trail.

As he took in gasps of cold air at the bottom of the trench, O'Connell looked over at Waller. The boy wasn't dead, but his color was unnaturally pale due to blood loss. O'Connell shouted for help, as his own wound dripped blood into the muddy belly of the trench.

13

BACK IN THE GAME

AFTER BEING WOUNDED WHILE SAVING MICHAEL WALLER, O'Connell met another Englishman he would come to have fond thoughts about. The man was a doctor named Richardson. It was his skill and knowledge that saved young Waller's life.

"What's that box for?" O'Connell asked the doctor. The man had rushed inside the bunker where O'Connell and Waller had been taken, while carrying a small wooden box. Upon spotting the box, O'Connell, who was lying on a cot, had raised himself up to one elbow.

"What's in this box may save that soldier's life," Richardson said, as he proceeded to remove a glass bottle, some tubing, and an assortment of odd-looking pieces.

The doctor performed a quick inspection of the bandages covering the bayonet wound on Waller and made a grunt of satisfaction over what he'd seen. Afterward, he checked on O'Connell's wound, then frowned.

"The medic who dug the bullet out of you could use some more training. You'll have quite a scar there once it heals."

"It hurts like hell too," O'Connell said. He then gestured at the contents removed from the box. "What is that?"

"It's a blood transfusion kit, and we're damn lucky to have one."

"I've read about that, you can use that to give Waller blood, yes?" O'Connell asked.

"Yes, and it will be your blood. You two are the same type."

O'Connell laid back on his cot. "Do whatever you have to but save that boy."

THE BLOOD TRANSFUSION WORKED. THE NEXT DAY, BOTH O'Connell and Waller were ferried to different French hospitals. O'Connell had expected to be back at The Western Front within days, but his leg wound had other ideas. The wound became infected, the infection spread, and O'Connell was in danger of losing his life.

O'Connell left the battlefield in September of 1918, wounded, but strong and vital. By October, he was thirty pounds lighter and walking with the aid of a cane. His struggle with the infection had been a long one, while his leg wound progressed slowly.

He'd been informed that Michael Waller survived, and had been promoted as well. O'Connell had also had his rank increased. He was a Sergeant and in line to receive a medal, his third. O'Connell worked hard to regain his strength and had replaced ten of the pounds he'd lost by the time his birthday rolled around in early November.

He soon learned that he was to return to the fighting within weeks. All that changed days later when the

Germans signed an armistice agreement with the Allies and brought the Great War to an end.

O'CONNELL WAS AMONG THE FIRST WAVE OF SOLDIERS discharged and found himself on a ship home on Thanksgiving Day. He stepped off the ship in New York harbor in the first week of December, having lost four of the ten pounds he'd regained, due to sea sickness.

After spending days reveling in the prodigious history section of the New York Public Library, O'Connell boarded a train and returned to Chicago just days before Christmas. He still walked with a limp, but his leg was on the mend and he had stopped needing the cane.

When he entered the office of Recti Construction wearing his uniform, Sergeant stripes, and medals, he could tell that it took Frank Recti a few moments to place him.

"Damn, Tanner, you look like hell."

"The war left me a little worse for wear, but I'll be my old self in no time."

"Let me know when that happens."

"You have work for me?"

"The Chicago Outfit has grown since you've been gone, and one of their men, Bruno Albertini, he's been bumping off my guys like you wouldn't believe."

"Pay me three grand and I'll clip him for you."

Recti laughed, and his wild hair seemed to move in all directions, as if he were standing amid a windstorm.

"No offense, Tanner, but Albertini and his guys would eat you alive in the condition you're in. He's got bodyguards around him at all times."

O'Connell grinned. "I've developed a new set of skills

since you last saw me. Tell me where I can find the target and he'll be dead by the end of the week."

BRUNO ALBERTINI DIED FOUR DAYS LATER WHILE SEATED IN a booth at his restaurant, with his six bodyguards and other mob soldiers around him. Blocks away, in the fourth-floor office of an insurance agency, O'Connell packed away his Springfield rifle and scope.

Tanner was back in town, and deadlier than ever.

14

A HIT MAN'S PARADISE

AMERICA DURING PROHIBITION WAS A BREEDING GROUND for many things. Among them, crime, fast money, and fear of a man named Tanner.

By the spring of 1920, Keane O'Connell had regained his full vigor and was offering his services to anyone with the money to pay him. There were many who availed themselves of his skills, as rival gangs formed to control the distribution of the illegal alcohol trade.

Twice, O'Connell was offered hits on Frank Recti, and he declined them both. It wasn't as if O'Connell felt he owed Recti anything, and the two of them were far from being friends, but Frank Recti had given him a lot of work over the years. O'Connell thought that should count for something.

The year 1920 had not been kind to Frank Recti and his fellow Black Hand members, as the Chicago Outfit became dominant among crime organizations. By October of that year, Recti's territory had shrunken to almost nothing, and he was down to less than a dozen men.

Desperate to regain power, Recti turned to O'Connell for help.

When O'Connell met privately with Recti in the mob leader's office and heard him out, O'Connell stared at the mobster as if he'd gone mad.

"You want me to bump off a man's family?"

Recti nodded. "And the man, and his top guys and their families too. A guy like you, I figure you could make it look like an accident, you know, a fire or something."

"I'm not a butcher and I don't kill innocents," O'Connell said.

There was a metal box sitting on the desk. Recti pushed it toward O'Connell.

"There's one-hundred thousand dollars in that box, Tanner. That's a hell of a lot of dough. It's all yours if you take care of this problem."

O'Connell pushed the box back toward Recti. "I'm going to give you some advice, Frank. Take that money and leave Chicago. If you don't leave soon, the Outfit will kill you."

Recti's face reddened. "Is that a threat? Has someone hired you to clip me?"

"I've already turned down people who want you dead, but there are other hitters, and if you were to do something like this... hell, man, even the bleedin' coppers might bump you off."

Recti waved a hand at O'Connell's last statement. "I own more cops than you can count."

"Maybe, but others own them too. Get out while you still can, Frank. I hear it's real nice down in Florida."

Recti stood in a rush. His face was still red, but his knuckles had whitened from the fists he was making.

"Get out of here, Tanner, and don't you dare warn the Outfit."

O'Connell stood and pointed a finger at Recti. "I don't give a damn about the Outfit, but if you or any of your men slaughter children you'll answer to me."

Recti moved his jacket aside, to reveal the gun on his hip. "Leave, Tanner."

O'Connell shook his head in disgust. He was amazed that Frank Recti would be stupid enough to threaten him. For a moment, he considered killing the man, but decided against it. The way Recti was going, he'd be dead any day.

O'Connell left the office without saying another word. He considered Frank Recti a part of his past.

$\sim$

DURING THE WINTER OF 1923 KEANE O'CONNELL TOOK A contract on a man who was said to be impossible to kill. The man's name was Gilberto Ricco, and Ricco was doing a good job of edging his way into the business of importing illegal alcoholic beverages.

He was even better at staying alive and had survived six different attempts on his life. The men who had attempted to kill him all died while trying. This included one who'd been sent back in pieces, after having been hacked to death by a meat cleaver.

Tanner agreed to take the contract for a flat fee of five-thousand dollars, which was a small fortune at the time.

Ricco was guarded by several dozen men, many of whom carried Thompson submachine guns. Ricco seldom left his home, and when he did, it was said he rode about in a car that had armor plating, with special glass that could withstand a shot fired directly at it.

O'Connell hadn't known that such a car could exist for personal use, but he had seen similar military vehicles during the war. Along with his fee, O'Connell asked for any information that was known about Ricco. To obtain more intelligence, O'Connell grabbed up one of the man's bodyguards, forced him to talk, then killed him.

With the information he'd gathered, he developed a plan to not only kill Ricco, but to ensure that he survive the aftermath of the hit. According to the bodyguard, Ricco had a huge shipment of booze coming in by boat on Lake Michigan. Ricco himself would be there to oversee the unloading and determine the quality of the product. Because of the recent attempts on his life, over fifty men would be on the shoreline, and along the roadways leading in to the area where the boat would offload.

There were also spotters already in place as a precaution against someone setting up an ambush, and several dirty cops would be on hand in case any civilians entered the area. In other words, any attempt to kill Ricco would be an act of suicide, and the shooter would likely never get close to the man.

~

KEANE O'CONNELL STEPPED ONTO THE ICE COVERING Lake Michigan and began walking in a southwesterly direction toward the shoreline of Chicago.

It was seven p.m. and he had to reach a spot over twenty miles away by first light on the following morning. The lake ice was thick, although hardly frozen over, given that the huge lake had a surface area of over twenty-thousand miles. O'Connell expected to make many detours along the way to avoid stepping on thin ice.

He carried a rucksack he had picked up while in the army. It held a change of clothes, some food, matches, a spare compass, and extra ammo, in the form of two five-round stripper clips. The ammo was for the Springfield rifle on his back. It had a Winchester scope attached and was wrapped in white cloth. Everything he wore had been dyed or painted white for the purpose of camouflage.

The moon was full and visible among drifting clouds, but the temperature was well below freezing. However, it was expected to climb to a balmy 24° by morning. O'Connell wore a ski mask, but he hated the thing. It was uncomfortable and made him itch.

He lit matches to read the compass he carried and found that he strayed off course often. Once, he had to walk miles out of his way, before finding ice thick enough to walk on.

When he was back on track, an arctic wind blew in from the north and the temperature dropped like a stone. O'Connell reasoned that such a fierce and biting wind wouldn't last long, not with the morning temperature expected to be in the low 20's, but the cold was debilitating. The wind was at his back for the most part, and he could feel his neck getting numb. He began to shiver and understood what that meant. The wind was sapping the heat right out of him. He needed to find shelter from it. But where?

After walking another mile, O'Connell saw a mound of snow that an earlier wind had formed. It was five feet high and twice as wide. The bitter wind had taken whatever snow had melted in the sun the day before and reformed that side of the mound into a wall of ice.

He walked around to the other side of the snowdrift and found refuge from the wind, while discovering that the drift was covering a damaged rowboat. The wood of the craft was only visible amid several bare patches. Someone had taken the small boat out on the lake and gotten caught up in the ice. That same ice had eventually shifted and crushed the modest vessel, which was later covered with snow.

Whoever the unfortunate mariner was who had owned the boat, O'Connell blessed them. He began feeling warmer without the sting of the wind, and decided to eat something, to take in a few calories and rest.

When he resumed his trek, he had been delayed for over an hour, but the wind had died down, and there was a glow in the east.

~

WHEN O'CONNELL FINALLY REACHED THE AREA OF HIS destination, it was after eight a.m., but to his relief, liquor was still being ferried ashore by rowboats from a ship.

There was a car parked near the trucks being loaded. From the description he'd received, O'Connell was certain he was looking at the armored vehicle containing his target, Gilberto Ricco.

The sight of the car buoyed O'Connell, who was exhausted from his long stressful trek over ice. But, he had determined that an approach to the shoreline from the lake was the only flaw in Ricco's defenses.

He assumed that the men guarding Ricco had deemed such a trek across the ice as impossible. It wasn't impossible; however, it was perilous and unsound. At any point along his tramp across the ice, O'Connell could have fallen through and never been seen again. O'Connell had been aware of the risk, but he had taken money to fulfill a contract and was willing to do whatever it took to complete the kill.

O'Connell unpacked the rifle with some difficulty since his fingers were numbed from the cold. His face hurt as well, and he couldn't feel his ears. The wind had picked up again, and the cold sliced like a blade. The hours of walking across the uneven terrain of the frozen lake had made walking a chore, and the soles of his feet were aching.

An hour later, he was still watching, still waiting, as the last of the cases were loaded onto the final truck. Ricco had not stepped out of his car or even opened his window. Meanwhile, it had begun to snow.

The snow was a blessing, in that it aided in camouflage, and it was a curse, as it made sighting in on the target more difficult.

O'Connell had been nearly a half mile from shore but had crawled closer as the snow developed.

The nearer he got to the shoreline, the thinner the ice became, and the greater the risk of falling through it and into the frigid lake water. O'Connell hoped that by lying down, it distributed his weight well enough so as not to stress the ice.

He tensed to take a shot when he saw a man in an Ulster coat with a fur collar approach the fortified vehicle containing Ricco. O'Connell was hoping for Ricco to step out, or at least open the door wide for the other man to get in, but no, the window only lowered several inches, so that they could speak.

Three photos of Ricco had been given to O'Connell along with his payment. They showed a swarthy man with bushy eyebrows and a thin moustache.

O'Connell never saw the moustache, but the bushy eyebrows were in his scope. He took in a breath of frigid air, held it, then released the breath as he pulled the trigger. The shot echoed over and across the frozen landscape, causing all who heard it to grow tense. The recoil of the rifle shifted his weight and the ice beneath his booted feet gave way. O'Connell's boots slipped into the water, but he dared not pull them out, or move in the slightest. Several men on shore had scoped rifles of their own. If they spotted movement, they'd fire at it.

He was certain his shot hit Ricco right between the man's bushy eyebrows and was pleased when he watched the man in the Ulster coat fall backwards and land on his ass. There was blood on the man's face, blood splattered from the corpse of Gilberto Ricco.

"Ricco's dead!" the man shouted. "His brains are all over the car."

More shouts came as everyone looked about for the shooter. O'Connell was relieved to see them looking in every direction but out at the lake. The driver was pulled from the front seat by a man who began beating him. The assumption being that he had killed their boss.

Then, one man took a rifle from an underling and began using his scope to peer out toward O'Connell's position. O'Connell had him lined up in his sights. If the man spotted him, he would kill him first.

A gunshot rang out, and the man with the rifle spun around, only to be shot in the stomach.

"Calavechi must have killed Ricco, but the bastard won't get away with it," the shooter cried.

He was then shot from behind, and his killer placed the blame for Ricco's death on another faction of their gang. With their leader dead, war had broken out between Ricco's lieutenants. In the confusion and chaos, O'Connell slipped away.

Two hours later, he walked ashore on a strip of ice and buried the rucksack and rifle beneath a snow drift, to be retrieved later. His wet feet had no feeling in them, so he hailed a cab and told it to take him to where he'd left his car, rather than walk another step. Back at his hotel, he summoned the house doctor, then took a long hot shower.

His feet were red, but feeling had returned to them accompanied by stinging pain. By the time the doctor showed up, O'Connell had eaten heartily, and blisters had formed on his toes.

The doctor, an older man with a jaded expression, told O'Connell to stay out of the cold while predicting a full recovery.

O'Connell thanked him, then ordered a bottle of champagne. Once his bottle arrived, O'Connell drank a glass of the bubbly in celebration of killing a man who everyone said couldn't be killed. Word would get around, and not only in Chicago, but across the country, as the mobsters and goons talked about the Ricco hit. They would ask who killed him, and the answer would be Tanner. Tanner had killed a man that no one else could.

O'Connell lofted his champagne flute up in the air, as a toast, but not to himself. He was toasting Tanner, his alter ego, Tanner, who was the best assassin on the planet.

"Fad saol agat," O'Connell said. It was a Gaelic toast which meant, "Long life to you."

On that snowy night in 1923, Keane O'Connell could have never imagined just how long-lived Tanner's life would be, and that the legend was just beginning.

15

DRAKE DIAMOND MOVIE FEST

Nadya had finished inserting a second Drake Diamond Blu-ray into the player when Florentina woke up. After she fed the baby, Sara and Amy took turns rocking Florentina until the child fell asleep again.

When the movie resumed, Amy brought out a bottle of wine, and the women settled in for another movie. By the time the movie ended, the bottle of wine was empty.

Spenser came up with a plan while watching Tricks move the stones aside. There was a thick section of trees nearby. Spenser walked among them while gathering up wood to burn in a campfire. While doing that, he made a phone call and found out that the Greene brothers were headed in his direction.

He had called a former client, a man he had rescued from a murderous loan shark. Spenser had a network of grateful clients who were happy to be able to help him when they could.

He never asked them for payment, instead, he took money or possessions from the people he saved them from. He once collected a small fortune from a hiding place in a drug kingpin's home, but he currently expected nothing from helping Andrea Jackson. The Greene brothers had been grabbed by the police before Spenser could get his hands on them, and so he felt he owed her one.

"It looks like the Greene brothers will be here sometime this afternoon," Spenser told Tricks as he dropped the wood he'd gathered. "They were spotted headed this way."

Tricks was panting from all the work he'd done, while his soft hands had gained budding blisters. After taking a long pull from a bottle, he spoke.

"You sure this plan of yours will work, Spenser?"

"It will if you run fast enough."

"What if they don't fall for your trap?"

Spenser considered Tricks' question, then he pointed at the hole where the rocks had been.

"Make that hole bigger. If they do kill you, then I'll have to bury three bodies."

"That's not funny, man."

"I know, with you dead I'll have to fill the hole back in by myself, and I hate grunt work."

Tricks glowered at him. "You're an asshole, you know that?"

"So I've been told, now, move more of those rocks… just in case."

Tricks went back to work while mumbling obscenities, and Spenser began building his fire.

∽

ROMEO SAT IN A CHAIR BESIDE ANDREA'S BED AND KEPT watch out a rear window of the home. There wasn't much to see other than trees and grass, yet off in the distance, beyond the abandoned superstore, was a section of the nearby highway. When Romeo used his binoculars, he could see that the traffic appeared to be light.

Andrea entered and smiled as she sat on the bed, facing Romeo. "You have one hell of a tan, Romeo, and I love your tattoos."

Romeo smiled back at Andrea. Her interest in him was obvious, and he found her attractive as well.

"I own a boat, so I get plenty of sun."

"You and Tanner, are you like Spenser?"

"What do you mean?"

"Spenser helps people who can't help themselves. Is that what you and Tanner do?"

"I'm just helping Spenser out for a day or two."

"And Tanner? He doesn't strike me as the helpful type. Actually, I think he's a little scary."

"Tanner's the best, but yeah, he doesn't help those who can't help themselves. You might say that he deals with those who *couldn't* help themselves."

"I heard you call him bro before. I guess it's just a name you call him, you look nothing alike."

"He's the closest thing I have to a brother."

Andrea reached out and ran a hand over Romeo's right bicep. "You certainly are in shape."

"And married," Romeo said.

Andrea removed her hand. "I saw the ring, but it's on your right hand."

"I live in Indonesia. We usually wear them on the right there."

Romeo took out his wallet. "Let me show you some pictures of our new baby girl."

Andrea laughed. "You really are married."

TANNER WAS WATCHING THE FRONT OF THE HOME FROM THE living room when Jasmine walked in and sat nearby. She held up her iPad, which displayed the cover of a popular book.

"Have you read this, Tanner? It's really good."

Tanner hadn't read the book, but he had once glanced over the description and passed on it. The book was about a man who discovered a way to travel between dimensions. The idea was that each time we made a choice, it spawned a new reality and a new world or dimension. Turn left at a stop light, and you're in one reality, turn right, and you're in another, different reality.

There was no one "real" reality, just an endless multiverse where countless copies of ourselves explored each and every possibility.

"I haven't read it, but I understand what the book was about," Tanner told Jasmine.

The girl smiled at him. "Do you believe it?"

"No."

Jasmine's smile went away. "You don't? Why not? It makes sense to me."

"I don't buy the concept because I believe in free will."

Jasmine looked confused as she tried to puzzle out Tanner's meaning. When she didn't see his point, she asked him to explain.

"How does this theory being true negate free will?"

Tanner smiled at her use of the word, negate. "You read a lot, don't you?"

"I do, and I'm a straight A student."

After giving the world outside another look of scrutiny, Tanner turned his head and spoke to Jasmine.

"According to this theory," Tanner said, while raising his right hand. "When I lift this hand, somewhere there's another me lifting the other hand, correct?"

Jasmine nodded her agreement.

"Doesn't that mean that the other me, the one who raised his left hand had to raise his left hand, as a reaction to my raising my right hand?"

"I guess."

"And if I decide to stand, there would have to be a me somewhere that remained seated, and he would exist in that seated position because I stood. If that's true, then these copies of me have no free will. They must act in a way opposite of the way I act, or I may have to act opposite of them."

Jasmine looked down at the floor as she worked her bottom lip with her teeth. Outside, a pickup truck parked across the street with two men inside. The men were black and muscular, but their faces were hidden in shadow beneath the bills of baseball caps.

"I understand your point," Jasmine said, "But the theory is looking at the numerous selves as one being, one whole."

"I'm not a section of a being," Tanner said. "I am myself, and the choices I make direct my life."

"Maybe that's just how it feels to us," Jasmine said.

One of the men left the truck and looked in Tanner's direction. In the man's hands was a Winchester rifle with a walnut stock.

"The theory says that every possibility is explored by the different selves, yeah?" Tanner asked, while never taking his eyes off the man with the rifle.

"Yes, that's what they say in the novel."

A boy ran from a house across the street. He called the man with the rifle, "Daddy!" then gave him a hug. Afterward, the man handed the boy his present, a new hunting rifle, a Winchester model 1866, nicknamed Yellow Boy, for its shiny brass receiver.

Tanner had failed to see the colorful gift ribbon along the barrel because the man had been gripping it. Tanner turned from the window as the truck drove off with the men and the smiling boy.

"If every possibility was explored, then there would have to be a you, a me, that never made a mistake, never turned right when they should have turned left, in other words, a perfect you, a perfect me. On the other hand, there would also be a you and a me who never did anything right, who made mistake after mistake. There's no one like that in either extreme, no one human. We are who we are, Jasmine, and we live with our mistakes, our failings. There's not a better copy of us somewhere. This is the life we get."

Jasmine closed the cover on her iPad, then gave Tanner a long look. "Maybe you should write a book."

"In a way I am," Tanner said. He was talking about the Book of Tanner, which he still had to make entries in upon his return to Spenser's home.

The sound of running footsteps came from the stairs, followed by Romeo appearing in the doorway.

"The kid's gone," Romeo said. "And his mother found a note."

16

TANNER ONE – 1923 – 1938

Prior to Prohibition, O'Connell had become friendly with a saloon owner named Jimmy Maloney. Maloney turned the saloon into a speakeasy during Prohibition and was a low-level member of the Chicago Outfit.

After having trouble with Frank Recti, O'Connell decided to do things differently. He set Jimmy Maloney up as a go-between for contracts. If anyone wanted to hire Tanner, they would have to go through Jimmy Maloney.

For his part, Maloney made out well financially in the arrangement, as O'Connell gave him a percentage of every contract. Hiring Tanner for a hit cost a flat, non-negotiable, two-thousand dollars. If the target was on the run or in hiding, the fee climbed to three-thousand. These were princely sums in the 1920's, but Tanner's reputation was well in place after his slaying of Gilberto Ricco. If you wanted a man dead, you hired Tanner.

Aspiring mob bosses and their men would have airtight alibis when the hit went down, and if the cops ever put the squeeze on anyone, all they could give them was a name,

Tanner. By the mid-1920's, the name Tanner was thought to be catchall by the cops. The Chicago P.D. believed no such man named Tanner really existed, and that it was just a name used by hoods when they were too afraid to point fingers at the true assassin. The name was also used by mob leaders to keep their troops in line.

"Anybody snitches to the coppers, and they'll get a visit from Tanner."

O'Connell found it all amusing. On average, he was killing five or six men a year, and yet, dozens of hits were being attributed to him across the country. Tanner was becoming a myth, like a boogeyman for mobsters.

But one man knew him by sight. That was Frank Recti. Recti had engaged in a street battle with the Chicago Outfit that had obliterated his men, however, Recti came out the other side still standing. It had cost him everything he had to save his neck, but by 1929, Frank Recti had redeemed himself and was a Made Man and a higher up in Al Capone's organization.

THE YEAR 1929 SAW THE ST. VALENTINE'S DAY MASSACRE, which soured public opinion and brought down new heat on mob activities. Meanwhile, dozens of rival gangsters were gunned down in the streets as chaos threatened to tear the Chicago Outfit apart.

A meeting was held in Atlantic City New Jersey in May of 1929, purportedly to bring about peace. In reality, it was an undertaking intended to dismantle Capone's hold on Chicago, by dividing his territory. Capone's activities were engendering scrutiny from federal authorities. That heat, if turned up high enough, would burn everyone, not just

Capone. When nothing changed, things only became worse, and Capone continued to reign.

It was in July of 1929 that Keane O'Connell visited a new rare book store. To his delight, the store had the six-volume set of Edward Gibbon's Decline and Fall of The Roman Empire. The books were in excellent condition. O'Connell purchased them, then arranged for the books to be delivered to the hotel where he was staying.

O'Connell had a picturesque home outside the city that no one knew of, but he stayed at hotels when working. He had made a hit the night before, the slaying of two men who'd been on the run from a Capone lieutenant. He had plans to return to his country acreage the following day.

The home was surrounded by rolling green hills that made him think of his boyhood home in Ireland. It was also dotted by ponds and bordered a lake on one side. O'Connell was forty-five, but other than his graying temples, he felt as fit and young as he ever had. The lake at the end of his property was four miles from his home, and O'Connell made the trek to and from the lake most days, while thinking.

He was an autonomous soul, a man who liked solitude, but the passing years and the lack of friends and family had left him feeling glum. There were days he missed his brother, Davin, fiercely, as well as the rest of his family, and he would drink and reminisce about better days and a youth long gone.

CHICAGO WAS A GROWING CITY IN THE 1920's AND construction often rerouted traffic. While taking one such detour, O'Connell drove past a storefront that sparked a memory. O'Connell was driving a red, Ford Model A sedan. After parking the vehicle in an alley by a movie theater, he walked back to the shop he passed, then stood outside to peer through the window.

He was at the dress shop where, twelve years earlier, he had left the waif, Eloise. There were three customers inside the dress shop; they were being waited on by a striking blonde. O'Connell looked the shop over but saw no sign of the girl he'd left there, while the blonde seeing to the customers looked nothing like the woman who had owned the shop. He sighed. Twelve years was a long time, and people moved on.

He returned his gaze to the blonde, and when he saw her smile, the truth struck him. The lovely blonde creature in the shop *was* Eloise. She had grown in height quite a bit, had shorter, well-styled hair, and alluring curves. It shocked O'Connell how different she looked, but he was thrilled to see her doing so well. When the customers left with their bundles of new clothing, O'Connell stepped into the shop.

"May I help you, sir?" Eloise asked.

O'Connell felt a pang of disappointment at not being remembered, but it disappeared as recognition lit Eloise's eyes and she rushed around the counter toward him.

"Tanner!"

Eloise hugged him as if he were a long-lost friend, and O'Connell laughed with pleasure at her joy.

"Hello, Eloise, and my, just look at you."

Eloise held up a finger, indicating to O'Connell that he should wait a moment. Afterward, she walked over to the door, locked it, and hung a sign that stated the shop was closed.

"Come into the back room, Tanner. We really must catch up."

O'Connell hesitated. "No, lass, I only stopped by to say hello. There's no need to lose business over the likes of me."

"Nonsense, Tanner. And I've an idea, it's lunchtime and I'm famished. Let's eat and we can talk over a meal."

O'Connell cocked his head. "You're sure about that, Eloise? Have you forgotten what sort of man I am?"

Eloise stood on her toes and kissed O'Connell on the lips. "You saved me from four men who were about to rape me, then you saw that I wound up somewhere safe. I know what sort of man you are."

O'Connell smiled. "I guess I could swallow a morsel or two."

ELOISE WAS UNMARRIED, BUT SHE HAD FALLEN HEAD OVER heels for a young accountant who had been classified as 4-F during the war. The man had been born with one leg slightly shorter than the other, which caused him to limp. Sadly, the young man later died during the outbreak of the Spanish Flu.

The woman who had owned the shop sold it two years earlier to Eloise for a bargain, then moved west to reunite with the daughter who had run off and eloped.

"I was only able to buy the shop because I still had that money you gave me, Tanner," Eloise told him.

Their long lunch was followed by a walk, then more talk back at the shop. O'Connell left Eloise that day with plans to return the following weekend. That one weekend became many, and O'Connell found that he was developing feelings for Eloise, feelings that she shared.

"I'm too old for you," he had told her after a shared kiss behind the closed doors of her shop.

"I'm not a little girl anymore, Tanner," she said, then she led him by hand up to her small apartment above the shop.

By the time the stock market crashed later that year, Eloise and O'Connell were seeing each other as frequently as they could, and he had told her his true name, and invited her to his home.

Keane O'Connell was happier than he'd been since leaving Ireland.

OLD FRIEND, OLD ENEMY

CHICAGO IN THE 1930'S WAS HIT HARD BY THE GREAT Depression, while the mob wars continued, and illegal booze kept flowing.

O'Connell began to work less. There were federal agents targeting the mob like never before and his go-between, Jimmy Maloney, had to reopen his speakeasy often, after being raided by treasury agents.

O'Connell didn't need the money. He had a paid for home on twenty acres, a safe full of cash, and simple tastes.

He also had Eloise, whom he had married in June of 1930. There would be no children from their union, as Eloise was incapable of having them. Her father had raped her while she was a child and had caused her damage. It mattered not to O'Connell. He had lost a wife and a son once because of a difficult pregnancy. He did not wish to tempt that agony again.

By the end of Prohibition in 1933, O'Connell was nearing fifty, but still took the occasional job. He had also upped his fee.

A contract he took in April of 1938 was on the leader of an emerging union in Detroit. The man was a con artist looking to cause trouble and hoping for a payoff to go away. It was a dangerous game, as the Detroit mob was strong. They were also under intense scrutiny, as were the unions they controlled, and so they brought in an outsider to handle the problem.

O'Connell attended a large union meeting outside a Detroit auto plant where his target would be speaking. He struck while the man was alone in a travel trailer he used as an office while touring. The young prostitute the union leader hired had just left the man lying in bed. O'Connell jimmied the trailer's cheap lock and killed the thug with a knife as he slept.

As he was walking away from the trailer, shouts rang out. O'Connell spun around with his hand on his gun, but the cries and shouts weren't directed at him. There was a man being chased by a small crowd of union workers who were armed with makeshift clubs.

Although he had only caught a glimpse of the man, O'Connell recognized him right away. The man was Michael Waller, who O'Connell had last seen gravely wounded during the war.

By the time O'Connell caught up to the crowd, Waller had decked three of the seven men, but three others had tackled him to the ground.

The remaining man was about to bring a two-by-four crashing down on Waller's head when O'Connell punched the man in the throat.

Seeing their companion drop to his knees and gag for breath, the men holding Waller released him to attack

O'Connell. That was a mistake. A short time later, Waller and O'Connell were the only ones standing.

Before they could reunite properly, more men came running toward them. O'Connell told Waller to follow him, and they were soon driving off in the car O'Connell was using. Once he was certain they weren't being pursued, O'Connell parked and grinned at Waller.

"It's good to see you again, lad."

Waller was rubbing sore knuckles. He also had a nasty bruise forming under his left eye.

"You're not as glad to see me as I am to see you, Keane. Those men might have killed me."

O'Connell nodded as he took a good look at Waller. As a boy, Waller had already been tall. He'd grown even taller and was a muscular man.

"Why were those men after you?"

"I'm a Pinkerton Agent. I was working undercover, and someone got wise. It was a man who knew me from another undercover job I'd done."

"I should have known you'd have a dangerous job, lad."

Waller smiled. "It keeps things interesting."

THE TWO MEN WENT TO A BAR AND CAUGHT UP. O'Connell felt bad lying to Waller, but he wasn't about to tell him the truth. Michael Waller was thirty-six. He had never married and had seen the country while working for the Pinkerton Detective Agency.

"I'm thinking of settling in Detroit. The city is growing like crazy and I like it there," Waller said. "But I'll be in your neck of the woods soon. I'll be training a new office opening up in Chicago next month."

"How long will you be there?" O'Connell asked, while lighting his pipe.

"Several weeks, we'll be starting from scratch."

"Then you'll have to come to dinner, and you can meet my wife, Eloise."

"I don't want to put you to trouble."

"It's no trouble, lad."

Waller grew serious and stared into O'Connell's eyes. "I owe you my life. If not for you, I'd have died in that French farmhouse and never made it home from the war."

"You'd have done the same for me, Michael."

Waller nodded. "I would have."

"I know it, lad. You're as brave and steadfast as they come."

~

WALLER ARRIVED IN CHICAGO A FEW WEEKS LATER.

Michael Waller had stayed in the army after the war, had trained as a medic, but found Army life boring during peace time. After returning to civilian life, he joined the Pinkerton Detective Agency. The work was exciting but paid little.

Eloise liked Michael Waller the moment she met him and saw a side of O'Connell she'd never seen before. O'Connell was a solitary sort, preferring his books to the company of others, and she had felt a sense of pride that he had allowed her into his life.

Waller was also allowed to see the human side of Keane O'Connell, and Eloise listened with rapt attention as the men discussed the war. Neither man spoke of the killing they had done, but Eloise read between the lines and thought that Michael Waller must be a very brave soul. Perhaps it was that quality that tied the two men together, bravery, and a sense of daring.

In any event, Eloise was happy to see that O'Connell had at least one friend in the world, for despite her presence in his life, at heart, Keane O'Connell was a lonely man still mourning his dead first wife, and infant son. She knew O'Connell loved her, and they were happy together, but Eloise understood that some wounds never quite healed.

CAPONE'S FALL AND IMPRISONMENT TURNED OUT TO BE A good thing for Frank Recti. Recti had risen even higher in the Outfit and was in control of the Outfit's enforcement of rules. O'Connell had heard rumors about Recti, which were passed along by his contact, Jimmy Maloney. Recti was said to be holding a grudge against Tanner.

"Word is, this team of hitters the papers are calling Murder Incorporated isn't doing as well as it should be here in Chicago. If people want someone hit, it's you they call. Frank Recti is saying that independent hitters are no good, because you don't answer to the Outfit. He came here asking me how he could find you."

O'Connell gave that some thought, then offered Jimmy Maloney advice. "You should leave town until some other bee gets in Recti's bonnet."

"I'm not worried about Recti, Tanner. Besides, I couldn't tell him where to find you if I wanted to. He knows that, and I got friends too."

"All right, Jimmy. I'll check in with you next week."

Six days later, Jimmy Maloney was dead. He had been shot inside his bar in what the police were calling a robbery.

∼

AFTER LEARNING OF MALONEY'S DEATH, O'CONNELL stopped at a drugstore to make a call. He spoke to a mutual acquaintance of Maloney's named Martin Hoffer. Hoffer was a bartender who worked at Maloney's bar.

"It was no robbery, Tanner. I found Jimmy. He had been tied to a chair and tortured. Someone had cut off his fingers and gouged his eyes out."

"Jimmy said that Frank Recti had been in to see him."

"Yeah, Tanner. This was done by Recti's people."

"Are you sure, Martin?"

"Yeah, I'm sure, because they paid me to keep my mouth shut."

"But you're talking to me."

"That's right, because if you're the kind of man I think you are. I know you'll kill that bastard Recti for what he did to Jimmy."

"Leave town, Martin, and don't come back until you hear that Recti is dead."

"I'll be on a bus out of town tomorrow morning, and Tanner, I ain't coming back."

O'Connell hung up the pay phone he had used. He left the drugstore, walked to a car parked at the curb, and climbed into the passenger seat. O'Connell had recently taught Eloise to drive, and she had driven them into the city.

"Do you have to work soon?" she asked. She always called what O'Connell did for a living "work" because that was the way he himself referred to it.

"No, dear, but I do have business to take care of."

"It wasn't just a robbery? Your friend Maloney was murdered?"

"Yes, by Frank Recti."

"I'd ask you to let it go, but I know you too well."

O'Connell heard the worry in her voice. He reached over and took her hand.

Eloise laid her head on his shoulder. "Killing this man, Recti, will it be dangerous?"

"Yes, because he'll be well-protected."

"Call Michael and ask him to help you."

"I can't do that. He knows nothing about my being Tanner. Besides, it's not his fight."

Eloise turned in her seat and threw her arms around O'Connell's neck. "Promise me that you won't die. I know it's silly of me to ask it of you, but I want to hear you say it."

O'Connell smiled. "I won't die, but Frank Recti is a dead man."

18

THE DISAPPEARING TRUCK TRICK

WYOMING, PRESENT DAY

TANNER HELD UP THE NOTE ETHAN HAD LEFT BEHIND. IT said that Ethan was going to a friend's house and would be right back.

"Is this another of the boy's jokes?" Tanner asked Andrea.

"No, Tanner. He really left to go to a friend's house. I told him he was to stay home today... but Ethan is headstrong."

Tanner handed Andrea the note. "This friend of his he mentions, Marcus, where does he live?"

Jasmine answered. "It's not far. Marcus and his sisters live at the end of Pine Street, but Ethan would take a shortcut by cutting across the parking lot of the store."

"That big store that closed down?" Tanner asked.

"Mm-hmm," Jasmine said. "If you want I can walk there and bring him back."

"No, I'll go get him," Tanner said, while putting on a loose-fitting jacket.

Tanner and Romeo spoke alone for a few moments, while they were talking, Andrea had made a call.

"Marcus's mother told me that Ethan just left their house. He went there to borrow a video game. He should be back in a few minutes."

"I'll still go out to meet him. Romeo will stay here and keep watch."

Tanner was opening the front door when Andrea called to him.

"I know Ethan's prank annoyed you earlier and that he shouldn't have gone out without permission, but my son's a good kid, really."

Tanner relaxed and sent her a smile. "I was a bigger pain at his age. I'll find him and bring him right home."

"Thank you."

THE CLOSED BIG-BOX STORE SAT SURROUNDED BY ASPHALT like a castle surrounded by a moat. Tanner came across Ethan in the rear parking lot. The boy appeared confused as he kept leaning over and studying a dumpster that was positioned in front of a brick wall.

When Tanner called his name, the boy looked startled. In his right hand, he gripped the game he had borrowed from his friend.

"C'mon, kid, and I'll walk you home."

Ethan blinked up at him. "I saw a truck disappear."

"Right."

"No, really Tanner. There was a moving truck in the parking lot headed this way, but when I walked over here it was gone."

"Maybe it disappeared like the two men who had been in your room."

Ethan shook his head. "I'm not lying… not this time. The truck really disappeared. It was a big truck, a white one," Ethan waved an arm around. "This lot is huge. If the truck drove off I would have seen it."

"Or heard it," Tanner said.

"Right, and I did hear it. I heard an engine, and it sounded like it was coming from over here."

Tanner stared at the boy. "You don't sound like you're lying."

"I'm not."

"All right, so it's a mystery, but let's go. I promised your mother I'd bring you home."

Ethan looked at the dumpster again, shrugged, and turned to walk home. When they reached the front of the store, Tanner saw three men walking out the glass doors of the entrance. The glass was heavily tinted and reflected like a mirror. One of the men wore a black clerical shirt with a white tab collar. He waved while smiling, and Tanner stopped to talk with him.

"Hello there, can we help you?" the man asked.

"We're just cutting through the parking lot."

"I went to a friend's house," Ethan said while pointing. "He lives on the other side of those trees."

The man introduced himself as Reverend Smith. The other two men just stared.

Tanner pointed at the building. "Are you turning this into a church?"

"We hope to, along with a youth center and a homeless shelter."

"That sounds like a lot of work," Tanner said, then he covered his mouth as if to stifle a yawn. When he put his hand down again, it was closer to the gun he wore on his hip. The gun was concealed by his jacket. "I wish you luck, Reverend, but we have to get back home."

"God be with you," Reverend Smith said.

Tanner placed a hand on Ethan's shoulder and moved the boy along in the general direction of his house, while doing so, he kept the reverend and his two friends in his peripheral vision.

In the reflection of the glass doors, Tanner had seen a gun tucked in the rear waistband of the reverend. He had also made out the outline of shoulder rigs on the other men, beneath their windbreakers. Once they were out of the parking lot and approaching the house, Tanner stopped and looked at Ethan carefully.

"Did a truck really disappear back there?"

Ethan nodded emphatically. "Yeah. I'm not lying, Tanner. I saw this white truck go around the side of the building, then I still heard it. But when I walked around to that side, it was just gone, and it couldn't have left the parking lot that fast."

"Okay, I believe you," Tanner said, but he had no idea what to make of it, or of the men with the guns.

TRICKS WAS IN THE SHOWER WHEN THE GREENE BROTHERS arrived. Several hours had passed since Spenser received the call saying that the men were headed their way. Tricks began to believe that they had gone elsewhere.

"It's been five years, Spenser, and if they kill me the cops will know they did it."

"They were your partners. Do you remember them being the forgiving type, or giving a damn about the law?"

Tricks had said nothing to that, then insisted he needed a shower.

"Not a good idea. If they show up while you're in the shower, you'll be a sitting duck."

"I'll take my chances, man. I have to get clean after moving all those damn rocks."

"Fine, but when they show up, follow the plan. If you do anything else I may not be able to protect you."

"The plan, right, I know. Shit, we rehearsed it six times."

Just minutes later, Tricks heard the engine of the Greene brothers' car and leapt from the shower to look out a front window. He was naked, covered in soap, and so scared that his knees shook.

"Spenser?"

No answer, but then Spenser's words echoed in his head.

"Follow the plan."

Tricks nodded as if Spenser was standing before him. He had to get outside to put the plan in play. The trouble was, there was only one door leading out of the trailer.

A voice boomed from outside. It was Daryl Greene. "Come on out, Tricks. It's us, Daryl and Kevin. We got out of prison and figured we'd look you up. You know, let bygones be bygones and all that shit. We just want to talk to you, no lie."

"Yeah, man," Kevin Greene said. "We got a sweet deal in the works down in Mexico and we want to cut you in on it."

Tricks knew they were lying. He ran toward the rear of the trailer with a towel wrapped around his waist. There was a rear window in the bedroom. It was damn small, but Tricks hoped he could squeeze through it. He eased it open without a sound, then stuck his head out of it.

With an effort, he squeezed his shoulders through, then he gripped the top edge of the aluminum window frame to get leverage.

The metal hurt his already blistered hands and Tricks worried about the noise that the flexing of the aluminum window frame made. His worry turned to panic when he heard the trailer door being kicked in. Tricks tried wiggling his hips to get them through the window, but the opening was too small.

"Where are you hiding you little shit?" Daryl Greene shouted.

Tricks heard the man's booming voice and his effort to escape became a frenzy of activity. His hips passed through the narrow gap as the window frame bent to accommodate them, but he lost his towel and landed outside naked among weeds.

"The plan. The plan," Tricks said as he sprinted away from the trailer. He was repeating the words like a mantra. He looked back over his shoulder and saw nothing. There were no faces in the window he'd fallen out of and the Greene brothers were nowhere in sight. Several seconds later, he looked back again, and released a sound of horror as he saw Daryl and Kevin running after him with a speed he could never attain.

The two brothers looked huge, massive, and had obviously been hitting the weights while in prison. They wouldn't need to shoot him, Tricks knew, they could each grab an end and pull him apart like a chicken wing.

Tricks damned Spenser once more for not allowing him to run and hide. He stumbled twice after stepping on rocks and opened up cuts on the soles of his bare feet, but he maintained his balance and kept running.

There was a copse of trees near the spot where he moved the stones. Tricks ran behind them and knew that he was out of view of Daryl and Kevin, just as he was meant to be. Then, according to the plan, he moved into position, then stopped, even though his natural instincts were telling him to keep running.

Tricks stood there, feet bleeding, naked, his chest heaving from his exertion, and watched as the Greene brothers slowed upon seeing him. They stared, as they saw Tricks standing behind a low campfire with billowing smoke rising from the unseasoned wood it burned. The hatred in their eyes was palpable, but Tricks attempted to smile.

"Hey, Daryl, Kev. Did… did you really just come here to talk?"

Daryl Greene smirked. "What do you think, asshole?"

The Greene brothers took out guns and began firing.

WHAT SORT OF MAN BE YE?

CHICAGO 1938

O'CONNELL STOLE A CAR FROM THE PARKING LOT AT THE train station and drove toward the construction company owned by Frank Recti. The construction company had grown over the years. Recti had moved his headquarters in 1932 after erecting a five-story office building in a different section of the city. The top four floors were rented out, although being the Depression, most of the offices were empty, and none of the tenants were around at night.

Recti Construction on the bottom floor showed signs of life, as O'Connell had expected it would. There were lights on in the front windows, although the green roller blinds were lowered, blocking the view inside.

O'Connell remembered that Frank Recti always worked late, or rather, the man had nowhere else to be. Recti had never married, had no children, and cared only about his construction business and making money.

O'Connell had seen the man's picture in the paper

recently. It had been taken at the grand opening of a movie theater that had been built by Recti Construction. O'Connell read in the papers that Frank Recti's construction company was doing well despite the downturn in the economy, no doubt with the help of bribes and coercion. The man still had that head of wild hair, only the hair had grayed.

O'Connell thought about his own hair, which was streaked with strands of white. Neither he nor Recti were young men anymore.

There was a car parked outside the front doors of Recti's building with two men sitting inside it. They were Recti's bodyguard and driver. The sight puzzled O'Connell. He had expected to see a hoard of men guarding Recti. He had assumed the man knew him well enough to know that he would come to kill him and would have prepared for an attempt on his life.

O'Connell drove past the building with a hat pulled down over his eyes. It was a Sunday night and the shops were closed, what few remained open that is. Eloise still owned the dress shop, but more and more she sat in it alone, without a single customer coming in. There was just no money for store-bought dresses.

Despite the massive government spending to fund New Deal projects, unemployment was high, and getting worse. People were cutting up old tires to patch their worn shoes, while apartments meant for two to four people were housing up to a dozen desperate family members.

Many of the businesses around Eloise's shop had closed, victims of the bad economy. O'Connell, a student of history, had bought up the properties for pennies on the dollar. He understood that economic depression, no matter how great, never lasted. When the economy recovered, he and Eloise would be sitting pretty.

He checked his watch. The Amos 'n' Andy program was on and most people were glued to their radios, looking for a laugh during the bleak times. There were few cars on the road, particularly in the business section where Frank Recti's building sat. O'Connell thought that a vehicle might give chase after he drove by, but no, he was not followed. After driving several blocks, he pulled to the curb, stepped out of the car, and gazed back toward Recti Construction while leaning on the car's trunk.

The man had to know he was coming, had to expect it, and thus, had to be ready for him. If he stepped one foot inside that building, there was every chance he would never walk out again. There was another factor to consider as well. Frank Recti was what the Chicago Outfit referred to as a Made Man.

That meant that he was untouchable. Made Men weren't to be harmed or killed unless permission had been granted by the Chicago Outfit's council. If a Made Man was slain without the council sanctioning it, then the perpetrator would be hunted down and killed, and likely tortured in the process.

O'Connell remembered hearing about one such man. He was found living in Nevada, years after committing the transgression. The story goes that he was taken out in the desert and tortured for over a week before dying. The man's wife and children also went missing, although no one knew if they had gone into hiding or been buried in the desert.

The bottom line was that killing Frank Recti meant trouble. O'Connell had to decide if Recti was worth it. Thinking about it dispassionately brought only one answer. No. Frank Recti wasn't worth losing a night's sleep over, much less the ruining of one's life.

And what had Jimmy Maloney been to O'Connell

anyway? Although friendly, they certainly had never been friends. Jimmy Maloney had been a conduit used for obtaining work. He had been well-paid for his trouble as well. O'Connell owed the man nothing. And hadn't he advised Maloney to leave town for a while? Yes, he had.

Killing Frank Recti wouldn't bring Maloney back. It would only bring a world of grief to O'Connell.

With a sigh and a shrug, O'Connell turned to get back in the car, but then froze.

Why had Frank Recti killed Jimmy Maloney? He had done so in an attempt to locate Tanner. Recti hated Tanner. He had hated Tanner ever since Tanner had stood up to him and refused to kill innocents.

Although Frank Recti's stature had grown over the years, so had Tanner's reputation. Recti saw Tanner as an obstacle in his plans to own the assassination trade. Recti wanted to be the go-to-guy for hits in the Chicago area. However, as efficient and deadly as his mob soldiers were, they were still just that, mobsters.

They were men with records, with mugshots, with a string of bad deeds and victims behind them. Tanner was a ghost, a quasi-legend, who killed and then disappeared. No one outside of Eloise knew that Tanner was actually a man named Keane O'Connell.

Yes, Tanner was a man, not a ghost. He was a man, and men bled, men died. And men, no matter how brave, experienced fear. O'Connell was fifty-three. Although in excellent condition, he was not a young man. He was slowing down, and the leg that had been wounded in the war sometimes ached for no reason.

He had been taking less jobs and traveling more with Eloise at his side. His was a good life. During a time when many men were standing in bread lines for their next meal,

O'Connell lived in a beautiful home which was surrounded by picturesque acreage.

A scholar by nature, he often spent hours in his home library enjoying his books, and fate had been kind enough to give him a beautiful woman to share it all with.

Yes, Tanner was a man, and that man was Keane O'Connell, but what sort of man ran from a fight? O'Connell shook his head. It would be madness to risk himself and all he had to live for. However, Frank Recti had killed Jimmy Maloney in part as a lure, as a dare for Tanner.

Recti believed that Maloney was Tanner's friend, and he had killed the man anyway. It was his way of telling Tanner that he didn't fear him, although Recti knew full well that Tanner was someone to fear. The murder of Jimmy Maloney was a challenge. It was Frank Recti's way of taunting Tanner.

"Look what I can do, Tanner," Recti was saying. "Look what I can do and know that there's not a damn thing you can do to hurt me in return."

Frank Recti was betting that he could kill Tanner before Tanner could kill him. And yes, the odds were in Recti's favor.

O'Connell turned back and stared in the direction of Recti Construction, as a fire ignited in his breast.

He was a man, yes, but what sort of man? Was he a cautious man? A man who weighed facts and considered every angle before acting? Was he ready to give up and let the world chip away at him?

In the old days, when gold was used as currency and coins were first made of the substance, bits of the coins were chipped away and melted into gold ingots. The smaller coins retained their monetary value, but they were no longer truly worth what they had been before being debased. O'Connell wondered if ignoring Recti would be the same as chipping a piece off himself, of debasing himself, and making himself less than what he was.

He had faced tough odds fighting for freedom in Ireland, while in the army, and when carrying out contracts. He had killed targets who were well guarded and had walked away unscathed. Wasn't Recti just another hit? Just another thug to be clipped? No, he wasn't, because Frank Recti knew his capabilities and would be ready for him the way that no other target ever had been.

A memory returned to O'Connell then, one that had taken place in Ireland. In 1902, he had been a bookish kid and a quiet lad, but he had also been a tough boy who enjoyed working the farm and hunting.

When a new family moved in nearby, the sons turned out to be bullies. They were the Donnelly brothers, Cormac and Brennan, and large young men they were. The Donnelly brothers put fear in most just by looking in their direction, and they had beaten up more than one unfortunate soul who dared to talk back to them.

One day, they came across O'Connell as he was leaving the general store. He had just purchased a new book of poetry. The general store was the kind of place where old men sat out on its porch and played board games or cards while telling lies about the old days.

The elder Donnelly brother, Cormac, who was the bigger of the two, snatched the book from O'Connell's hand, then brayed with laughter when he saw what it was.

"He's reading poetry," the thug said, declaring it as if the book were about a taboo subject.

O'Connell was only seventeen at the time, and a head shorter than either man. Without hesitation, he demanded that he be given his book back.

One of the old men on the porch spoke up. It was said

that he was a hundred if he was a day.

"Give the lad back his book now. He's the sensitive sort he is."

The old man had been trying to help, but the Donnelly boys roared with laughter. Cormac Donnelly tore the book in two with his ham-sized mitts, then tossed the pages at O'Connell's feet.

"Let's see if we can make the sensitive lad cry," Cormac said.

O'Connell looked down at his book, and when he raised his head, he locked eyes with Cormac Donnelly. The big man saw something in O'Connell's gaze that made the look of mirth leave his face.

Brennan, the younger brother, hadn't glimpsed the fire in O'Connell's eyes, as his brother had, and he reached out with both hands to shove him.

O'Connell gripped Brennan's fingers while thrusting a knee into his midsection. Brennan bent forward as the air left his lungs. While still gripping his fingers, O'Connell gave them a vicious twist, dislocating several of Brennan's digits.

Cormac threw a punch at O'Connell's head, but he was as slow physically as he was mentally. O'Connell let go of Brennan's hands and sent a series of blows at Cormac, most of which connected with his nose.

O'Connell avoided a roundhouse punch by ducking under it and followed that with a hard uppercut to the side of Cormac's head. The blow stunned the behemoth and he dropped to one knee. As he struggled to get up, O'Connell busted his nose, then kicked him in the chest, sending him sprawling backwards.

Brennan bellowed with rage and charged at O'Connell. O'Connell met his charge with one of his own and sent stiff fingers into the man's throat. That took the fight out of Brenan, who gagged and moaned that he couldn't breathe.

"If you can talk, you can breathe," O'Connell told him, then kicked him on the side of the head.

As O'Connell was picking up his ruined book, Cormac Donnelly made it to his feet. Blood dripped from Cormac's broken nose and ran down his shirtfront. O'Connell stared at him, daring him to fight again. The big man had had enough. He helped his brother up, and the two of them staggered away.

O'Connell heard a chair scraping on wood as it was pushed back. When he turned to look at the porch, he saw the old man who had spoken earlier. The arthritic man struggled up from his seat to lean on a gnarled wooden cane. He stared at young Keane O'Connell as if he were an enigma. He had thought O'Connell a gentle soul but had viewed his ferocity when provoked.

The old man tilted his head and asked a question. "What sort of man be ye, lad?"

O'Connell grinned at the old-timer. "I'm the kind of man who doesn't run from a fight."

THIRTY-SIX YEARS LATER, KEANE O'CONNELL STARED OFF into the distance as he remembered that day. He then closed his eyes and came to a decision. When his eyes opened, he was Tanner, and only Tanner.

Tanner smiled and made a gun with his fingers. After pointing in the direction of Frank Recti's office, Tanner dropped his thumb in a pretense of pulling a trigger. "Bang!"

He laughed as he got back into the car and headed off to kill Frank Recti.

A MAN LIKE NONE OTHER

ON THE ROOF OF A BUILDING ACROSS THE STREET FROM Recti Construction, Tanner slid an icepick into the base of a man's skull, then he gave the makeshift weapon a violent twist.

The sniper fell toward the roof along with the rifle he'd been holding. Tanner caught the rifle, but let the man drop. The rifle was Russian-made, a Mosin-Nagant M91. Tanner took it with him as he headed back down the fire escape. The rifle had a strap and hung across his back.

He reached the alley at the side of the building in less than a minute. The climb up the fire escape had taken considerably longer, as he'd had to remain silent and go undetected. There had been two snipers, and the other one was just as dead as the man he had killed with the icepick.

Tanner returned to his stolen car. He had found a gas station that was still open out on the highway and had filled his tank. He put the icepick to work once more, by crawling beneath the car and opening a gash in the side of the fuel tank. Afterwards, he climbed into the car and drove toward the glass front doors of Recti's building.

The driver and bodyguard stood out in front of the building while smoking cigars. They gawked at Tanner as he turned his steering wheel sharply, jumped the curb, and sped toward the glass doors.

The doors gave way, but their metal framing slowed the vehicle, and Tanner thought a part of his plan might not work. He had aimed the car at a display case on the left of the lobby, where miniature models of several buildings were on view. Tanner wasn't interested in the models, but he needed to have the driver's side of the vehicle sitting astride the base at the bottom of the display case. The tilt would cause the fuel leaking from the gas tank to flow toward the office, and he was counting on the gas to help even the odds.

The impact with the doors had been tremendous, but Tanner had been ready for it. The metal doorframe gave way and Tanner recovered his balance by the time the driver-side tires came to rest on the base of the display. He grabbed up the weapons he had on the seat, rolled out of the car, and brought up one of the guns to fire, as a bullet pinged off the vehicle's roof.

Tanner had already been aiming at the man who'd fired the shot. It was the bodyguard who had been standing outside with the driver. Tanner fired several shots from the Thompson submachine gun he was holding and ventilated the bodyguard and the driver. Before the men's bodies fell, Tanner turned and emptied the rest of the magazine at the doorway of Recti's office, where several men had just stepped out.

Tanner then dropped to the floor, grabbed up a second Thompson, and fired at the legs of the next group of men to leave Recti's office. They fell amid cries of pain and Tanner changed the magazines on both weapons.

He stood then, ready to advance on the office and kill

Frank Recti, but a bullet ripped through his left side. Tanner fired the Thompson even as he spun around to drop to his knees. There had been a man hidden on the landing of the stairs, and Tanner caught him in the stomach right before the gun ran dry.

The man dropped his rifle, which slid down the stairs, then he crawled out of view to a corner of the landing.

When Tanner looked down at himself, he was shocked by how much blood he'd already lost. He had little time to assess his wound, as more men slipped from the office. They peppered the vehicle Tanner was behind and bits of glass and leather flew about. The elevator chimed, disgorging more men. Within moments, Tanner was outnumbered a dozen-to one.

"Take him alive if you can. I want to torture the bastard." Those words came from Frank Recti. Who was staying out of sight in the office.

Tanner popped up and sent a short burst of gunfire at the office. This time his target wasn't the open doorway, but the plaster wall beside it, as Tanner tried to guess from where in the office Recti's voice had originated. There was a yelp from beyond the doorway. Tanner smiled, hoping he had hit Recti somewhere vital, but Recti's next words dispelled that notion.

"My ear! The bastard shot off a chunk of my ear. Fuck taking him alive. Kill that bastard. Kill Tanner!"

Tanner reached into his pocket and removed a wooden match, after flicking it with his thumb to ignite it, he tossed it beneath the car.

The tendrils of gasoline that had spilled across the lobby floor gave birth to flames and several men started screaming. Tanner bolted for the space where the lobby doors had been, as behind him, Recti's men were in a panic over the spreading fire.

Once outside, Tanner felt a wave of weakness come over him. When he looked down, he saw that his left pant leg was turning red from his own blood. He would die if he didn't take care of the wound in his side and stop the bleeding.

He took in a deep breath and headed for the car parked at the curb. Relief swept over him when he saw that the driver had left the keys in the vehicle. His pant leg was so wet with blood that the seat beneath him made a squishing sound as he sat. He had to get away, had to find a doctor, and he had to do it without being followed.

The rear windscreen exploded as shots from a revolver blew it apart, but Tanner already had the car moving. The revolver was joined by a machine gun, and Tanner felt the impact of the bullets as they ripped apart the seat back on the passenger side. The tires on that side of the vehicle went flat, and Tanner had trouble controlling the car as he made a right turn at the next corner.

He reached behind him and winced when he felt the jagged exit hole the bullet had made above his hip. The wound was leaking blood with every beat of his heart. He forced himself to grow calmer, to slow his pulse.

That lasted for only seconds, then he caught sight of a car making the same right turn he had made, only the other vehicle was moving so fast that it took the turn on two wheels. That car was followed by another set of headlights, and the vehicles closed in on him while riding abreast of each other. They were in a business district on a Sunday night, no vehicles were parked along the curbs, and they had the street to themselves.

Tanner had no doubt that Frank Recti was in one of the vehicles pursuing him, and given their speed, they would catch up to his damaged car in no time. He had two choices, stand and fight, or run and hide. Recti would be expecting him to run and hide, but Recti was the target, the prey, not the hunter.

Tanner stomped on the brakes and nearly flipped his vehicle as he attempted a tight turn that spun the car around. The un-inflated rubber on one wheel came off, but the others caught traction.

He pushed the limping Packard to its maximum speed and headed back toward the men chasing him, while leaving sparks in his wake. As he neared them, Tanner fired the Thompson submachine gun, destroying his windshield. The gun seemed much heavier than it had earlier.

His boldness worked. One of the cars veered away and slammed into an abandoned storefront. The entire vehicle entered the shop. Tanner thought it looked as if it had been swallowed by Jonah's whale.

Someone in the other vehicle fired out the back window as he drove past, and Tanner felt a stinging sensation beneath his right shoulder. He'd been hit again.

The slug had passed through the seat and embedded itself in a back muscle. When he reached behind to touch the area, he could feel the metal slug beneath his torn skin.

Once again, the chase was on, but now it was one on one. The Packard was listing to one side and Tanner had to struggle to keep the car from running up on the sidewalk. The vehicle behind him had turned and was rocketing toward him. Tanner waited until the car's headlights illuminated his interior, then he slammed on his brakes.

The driver behind him reacted with lightning speed, but in the instant it took the man to brake, he had covered the distance between them. A body flew out of the windshield of the car behind Tanner and landed on the trunk of the Packard. The thud of flesh hitting steel jarred

Tanner, rousing him. He had hit his head during the crash and had been disoriented.

As he scrambled out of the car and onto the Packard's hood, Tanner saw Frank Recti limping his way toward him in the distance, identifiable by the outline of his wild hair. Recti must have been in the vehicle that had crashed into the shop. Two other men were with Recti, one of whom was carrying a shotgun.

Tanner had lost the sniper rifle when it slid beneath the seat of the Packard. The machine gun was empty, and there was no time to switch magazines, but he still had a loaded pistol, a Walther. He fired at the two men who had survived the crash with the Packard. Their brains leak out onto seats that were already red with their blood.

Recti and the other men shot at Tanner with their Tommy guns, but they were too far away and the slugs from their choppers went wide or fell short. That wouldn't remain the case, as they were moving in on him fast.

A wave of dizziness washed over Tanner. It was the blood loss. He moved on unsteady legs toward a service station and kicked open the office door just as a bullet shattered the window beside him.

Tanner entered the shop and moved toward the garage where the work was done. There were no vehicles inside, and everything smelled like grease. A form flitted briefly past a small dust-covered window. It was one of Recti's men moving to the rear of the shop to block Tanner's exit out that way.

Tanner lowered himself behind a massive steel toolbox and loaded his last magazine into the Thompson.

Recti called out to his two remaining men. "There's a puddle of blood in the car. Tanner is bleeding like a stuck pig." It was true. And Tanner was growing weaker with each passing minute.

The handle on the back door jiggled and Tanner turned his head to look at it. As he did so, the sound of glass crunching underfoot came from the counter area. Tanner was trapped and outnumbered, but as his eyes adjusted to the darkness, he came up with a plan.

"Mikey?" Recti called.

"Yeah?" came a reply from behind the rear door.

"We rush him on the count of three. Kill anything that ain't us."

"He's a dead man now, boss," Mikey said.

Tanner fought against another wave of dizziness, gripped the Thompson, and waited to triumph or die.

TRENCH WARFARE

RECTI REACHED THE COUNT OF THREE AND TANNER HEARD the man at the rear kick in the door. Recti and his other man both carried machine guns with huge ammo drums attached.

They fired in a cross pattern while the man at the rear door used a pump-action shotgun to fire into the deeper shadows of the garage.

Frank Recti ran dry first, then squinted about as he searched for Tanner's corpse. The other machine gun ran out of ammo the same time that the man at the rear door used his last shell. The holder of the shotgun was a stocky man with a moustache. He was bringing out a loaded pistol when Tanner fired a burst at his head. The rounds all but obliterated the man's skull.

The other man with Recti turned to run and Tanner shot him in the back. Recti had seen where Tanner was firing from and had freed a gun from a holster on his belt. He never got to use it. Tanner stitched a line across Recti's stomach and the mob boss's weapon went flying.

The garage had a pit in its floor that was used by the mechanics to work on cars. A different kind of mechanic had put it to use and accomplished a different sort of work. It was reminiscent of the battles O'Connell had fought while in the trenches in France.

Tanner climbed out of the pit after three attempts. His strength was waning, while his vision was blurry. He picked up the gun Recti had dropped and shot the other wounded man, killing him.

Recti lay on his back, still alive, but with his eyes clenched and teeth gritted against the agony of his wounds. The left ear looked deformed and bloody from the damage one of Tanner's earlier shots had caused. Recti opened his eyes when Tanner pressed the man's own gun against the middle of his forehead.

"Million... A million dollars if you let me live," Recti said.

Tanner said nothing, and in his silence, he gave an answer.

"Everything! Tanner I'll give you everything I have just don't pull that—"

The impact of the bullet made Recti's head bounce off the oil-stained concrete floor and the gun slipped from Tanner's grasp.

Tanner felt weak, exhausted. He had just leaned against a wall when he heard footsteps coming from outside. There was another man left. Tanner bent down to pick up the gun again but kept going. He hit the floor and landed beside Frank Recti. He was spent and lacked even the energy to turn his head to view the man who would kill him.

Keane O'Connell closed his eyes, and as he did so, he remembered the words of his brother.

"One good thing about dying," Davin had said. "I'll soon be with those who went before me."

O'Connell held on to that thought as he felt himself slipping away.

SMOKE AND MIRRORS

Sara, Amy, and Nadya took a break from their movie marathon to play with Florentina.

The baby loved the attention from her "aunts" and stayed awake longer than usual before succumbing to sleep. With her daughter asleep once more, Nadya put on another movie, while Sara made popcorn and Amy brought out a second bottle of wine.

When Drake Diamond came on screen again, this time playing an undercover cop working on a nude beach, the women stared at the screen with rapt attention.

"Um-um-umm," Amy said, and Sara and Nadya laughed.

Two hundred yards behind Tricks' trailer, faces that had been twisted by hate scrunched up in befuddlement. Daryl and Kevin Greene had fired a barrage of shots at Tricks, while meaning to kill him.

Instead, they made Tricks disappear amid the sound of glass breaking.

Their shots had shattered the large mirror that had previously been suspended over Tricks' bed, and in which they had viewed his reflection standing within a haze of smoke. Before the men could puzzle out what had happened, a shotgun roared and ripped them apart with 00 buckshot.

The Greene brothers fell to the ground and writhed in agony. Their pain was short-lived, as two more blasts from Spenser's shotgun ended their lives, and the threat they had posed. Tricks let out a hoot of triumph, before walking over and staring down with a solemn expression at the ravaged and unmoving bodies.

"Damn. When you're dead, you're really dead."

"That's how it works," Spenser agreed.

He told Tricks to go inside and put on some clothes, then to come back out so that they could bury the bodies beneath the rocks.

"When you say that we'll bury them, you really mean just me, right?" Tricks asked.

Spenser answered while putting on gloves. "I'll drag them over to the hole and you can cover them with stones."

Tricks sighed as he looked down at his hands, which were already blistered and sore. "I think I'll get some gloves too."

Tricks went limping off toward the trailer, as behind him, Spenser grabbed the ankles of Daryl Greene and dragged him toward the hole that would be the man's grave.

～

WHEN TRICKS RETURNED WEARING FRESH CLOTHES AND A pair of cotton gloves, Spenser saw that his mood had lifted. An illegal pharmaceutical was no doubt responsible for his mood change, but Spenser suspected that there was another contributing factor.

His suspicion was confirmed after the bodies had been buried, when Tricks waved off Spenser's warning to stay away from Andrea and the children.

"That's my family, Spenser."

"You lost the right to call them that when you ran off leaving them to die. Even your children don't want anything to do with you."

Tricks shook his head as he grinned. "I know Andrea inside and out. Once I turn on the charm, she'll let me back into her bed."

"If that happens, you'll receive a visit from me."

"You don't scare me, man. Andrea sent you here to save me from the Greene brothers. She's not going to turn around and let you hurt me."

"I don't have to lay a finger on you, but you will stay away from Andrea, or else."

"Or else what?"

Spenser brought out a cheap phone, then cued up a video. Once the film was playing, he turned it around to let Tricks look at it. The video showed Tricks hard at work, as he piled rocks over the bloody bodies of Daryl and Kevin Greene. Lying nearby was a shotgun.

"Bother Andrea again and the cops get this video," Spenser said.

Tricks was mumbling curses and looked mad enough to kill Spenser. Spenser didn't care. Over the years, better men than Tricks had tried their damnedest to kill him and failed. A hard look from a scumbag like Tricks didn't matter at all. As Spenser walked off toward the vehicle he had hidden out of sight, Tricks called to him.

"What do I do with the car the Greene Brothers arrived in?"

"That's not my problem," Spenser said, and he meant it.

He was putting Tricks out of his mind and thinking about how good it would be to get back home and enjoy being around his family and friends. It was a pleasure that Tricks' cowardice and abandonment of his own family had cost him forever.

THE RULES OF TANNER

NEAR CHICAGO, 1938

WHILE SEATED OUTSIDE THE HOME OF KEANE O'CONNELL, Michael Waller read the newspaper accounts of what reporters were calling a "mob war", while trying to wrap his head around the revelations he had discovered about his friend.

He knew Keane O'Connell was adept at killing, having fought beside him in the Great War, but an assassin for hire? It didn't seem to fit the gentle and scholarly man he had broken bread with recently.

O'Connell had killed fourteen men while wounding nine others.

It was no wonder the police thought the men had been attacked by a group. Two of the wounded were talking, telling tales of an assassin named Tanner who attacked their boss, Frank Recti, after Recti had killed a friend of Tanner's.

The police superintendent told newspaper reporters

that Tanner was a mob myth, nothing more than a hoax to keep the young mobsters in line.

"I would say that Recti and his gang had been attacked by no less than two dozen men," the superintendent stated. "Although we've yet to identify which rival gang was to blame."

When he was questioned about the fact that no members of a rival gang were found at the scene, the superintendent ended the interview.

Michael Waller set the newspaper down and stared out across a green field awash in sunlight as he pondered what it must have been like for O'Connell to go up against so many men alone. Waller was also a warrior at heart, and a smile crossed his lips as he thought about O'Connell's sheer audacity and daring.

"Glorious, it must have been glorious."

KEANE O'CONNELL AWOKE TO A VISION OF THE SUN filling his bedroom window, then found that he couldn't decipher whether the sun was rising or setting. He felt groggy until the pain on his left side came to his attention, and he released a moan.

Someone stirred in a chair beside him. It was Eloise. Her face was alight with joy at seeing him awake. After kissing him on his dry, chapped lips, she spoke.

"Thank the Lord you're awake, Keane. How do you feel?"

O'Connell attempted to speak, but only a croaking sound came out. After moving his tongue around a bit and clearing his throat, he could speak.

"My left side aches. I was shot there."

Tears ran down Eloise's face. "It was a bad wound and you lost so much blood, but Michael saved you."

"Michael? You mean Waller brought me here?"

"I know you told me not to do it, but I called him anyway. When he went to Frank Recti's place of business he said he found a scene of destruction and a blaze, then he heard gunfire in the distance and followed the sounds. Michael said he managed to get you inside his car and drive off right before the police showed up."

"So, he knows I'm Tanner?"

"Yes, and he saved your life. He broke into a clinic to get the supplies he needed, then he stitched your wounds. When I first saw you I... oh, you were so pale, Keane. I begged Michael to take you to a hospital, but he refused. He said that other mobsters would try to kill you there, and that even if you lived, you'd be locked up for life."

"He was right, and I'd rather be dead than imprisoned."

"After Michael gave you his own blood, your color improved, but you slept away the day."

O'Connell looked out the window and saw that the world looked less bright than it had.

"Where is Michael now?"

"He's out sitting on the porch... with a bottle of whisky."

"Is he drunk? He shouldn't be drinking if he gave me his blood."

"No, he's far from drunk, but I think he's been unsettled by everything that's happened."

"Send him in here please."

Eloise leaned over the bed and kissed O'Connell again.

"I love you, Keane. Please don't do anything so foolish again."

"I likely won't have to. After what happened to Recti

145

and his minions, many will think twice before crossing Tanner again."

A FEW MINUTES LATER, MICHAEL WALLER ENTERED THE bedroom and sat where Eloise had been. He shook his head in wonder as he stared at Keane O'Connell.

"I never pegged you as an assassin."

"Why not? It's work like any other, Michael, and the killing is more honorable than the butchery we did during the war. In Chicago, I kill mobsters who deserve what they get. On the Western Front, we were killing shopkeepers, farmers, and clerks, men who had never harmed anyone, but just had the misfortune of being on the wrong side of the trenches."

Waller sat in silence as he considered O'Connell's words. He then moved aside the blanket covering O'Connell to check on his wound. The bandage was wrapped around O'Connell's waist. It was white, with only a spot of blood marring it at the rear.

"How much pain are you in?"

"It hurts like the dickens, and so does my back."

"You were shot twice, but the bullet at your back did little damage. It's a good thing for you I was an Army medic."

"You saved my life, Michael, and you've kept me from going to jail. Thank you, lad."

"You're welcome, but what now?"

"What do you mean?"

"Will men come after you?"

O'Connell considered the question, then smiled. "The man I went after and killed, Frank Recti, he was what the mobsters call a Made Man. No one is supposed to kill a

Made Man without being sanctioned by their commission. Oh, they'll want my head for breaking their rules, but I'm not one of them. As Tanner, I'm an outsider."

"Is there any way they can find you?"

"I don't believe so. I used a go-between for years. Recti and a few of his men know me by sight, but most of them are dead, or possibly in prison. Unless I stick my head up, they'll have no way to take revenge."

"Still, I'd feel better staying close to you for a while."

"What about your work with the Pinkerton Agency?"

"That's over. The new man at the top wanted me to be strictly a trainer, which is fine, and came with more money, but it would bore me. I like working in the field, being undercover, where I'm essentially my own boss. After a short rest, I guess I'll hook up with another agency."

O'Connell stared at Waller. "Now that you know about Tanner, do you think less of me?"

"That depends on who you've killed."

O'Connell scowled. "What do you think, boy, that I'd knock off some housewife for an unhappy husband?"

Waller sighed. "I wondered, yeah."

"As Tanner, I lived by a set of rules. I made money for killing, yes, and damn good money, but I never went against my code."

Waller reached over and squeezed his friend's shoulder. "I should have known that. I apologize for thinking otherwise."

Several days later, O'Connell was strong enough to go for a walk on his land.

Michael Waller accompanied him. It would not be the

long stroll to the lake and back that O'Connell was accustomed to, but he still felt good being out of the house.

At one point, a strange sound was heard overhead. When they gazed skyward, O'Connell and Waller saw an object with wings that was about half the size of an automobile.

"What is that?" Waller asked. "Is that a plane?"

"They call them model airplanes," O'Connell explained. "My neighbor on the other side of the lake flies them. That must be one of his. It's controlled by radio waves and uses petrol like a car."

"What does he do with it?"

"It's just a hobby, an expensive one would be my guess. I've seen him crash two of the noisy buggers into the lake while I was out on walks."

AFTER TRAVELING ABOUT A MILE ON THEIR TREK, WALLER suggested that O'Connell rest before heading back. The exertion had caused O'Connell to sweat, even though it was a cool day.

They rested near a pond. As the two men sat with their backs against a tree, Waller asked his friend a question.

"I remember you telling me that you lived by a set of rules when you acted as Tanner. What were those rules?"

O'Connell repositioned himself against the tree until he could look at Waller better. It also put less pressure on the small wound on his upper back.

"The first rule is to survive. If you think you can't kill your target and still get away clean, then come up with another plan. I always wanted Tanner to be exactly what he's become, part-ghost and part-myth."

Waller smiled. "You speak of Tanner as if he's another man."

"He is, Michael. Tanner is a creation, one that's evolved over the years. As myself, Keane O'Connell, I never would have gone after Frank Recti, not given the odds I faced. But those men weren't facing me, they were going up against Tanner, and they had all heard stories about him."

"Still, you *are* Tanner, Keane, and his boldness and skill at killing come from you."

"True, but it's like it was in the army. The enemy didn't fear me, a lone soldier, but they had nightmares about the faceless, nameless sniper I'd become."

Waller nodded slowly. "Ah, yes, I think I see your point. Even though you're Tanner, Tanner still exists as a being of his own, at least in the mind of others."

"Correct."

"What other rules were there?"

"Rule number two—Never kill the innocent. Rule number three—Kill the guilty, and make an honest dollar doing it."

Waller raised an eyebrow. "An honest dollar?"

"Killing is work, much the same as other work. It takes planning, effort, and skill."

"Any other rules?"

"Number four—Never leave an enemy alive, kill him before he has a chance to kill you. I foolishly failed to apply that rule to Frank Recti, and I'm paying for it now with pain."

"What's the next rule," Waller asked.

"Rule number five, the final rule—Never give up until the target is dead. I once had to track a man into Mexico to kill him. It took months and cost me more than I'd been paid to do it, but I'd been hired to kill him, and kill him I did. When Tanner takes a contract to kill, you can consider the target dead."

"Five rules then, and they all make sense, but I'd add a sixth one," Waller said.

"What's your sixth rule?"

"Be the best. Tanner is the best, Keane. Despite the police statements in the paper, they know that only one man was responsible for the killing of Frank Recti and his men. The thugs on the street know as well. Tanner is not only considered a ghost and a myth, but also a legend."

"How do you know that?"

"I still have friends at Pinkerton, men who work the streets. They say the members of the Outfit's council have all increased their security. They're afraid that Tanner may come after them."

O'Connell laughed, then winced, as his wounded side ached. "Killing Frank Recti was good for business. I bet I could double my fee. It's too bad I'm retiring."

~

WALLER STAYED WITH O'CONNELL FOR TEN DAYS. AFTER seeing his friend in a new light, Waller was interested in understanding as much as he could about O'Connell's alter ego, Tanner.

O'Connell spoke freely to Waller, and over time, he revealed the tactics and strategies he had developed through the years. When he recounted the tale of how he had killed Gilberto Ricco, Waller shook his head, as an amazed look covered his face.

"Walking on lake ice is risky as all hell, Keane. You were lucky that trek didn't kill you."

"Luck played a part, such as finding that mound of snow to crawl behind. But Michael, I never felt more alive.

I was out to kill a man who everyone believed couldn't be killed. When I accomplished that and lived, I knew I was the best. It's a rare thing to be the top in any field. It is an exceptional feeling."

Waller stared at O'Connell. "I can understand that. You should be proud."

"I am," O'Connell assured him.

THE VACUUM LEFT IN THE MOB'S HIERARCHY DUE TO THE elimination of Frank Recti turned into a power struggle between rivals. When the dust appeared to have settled, the man at the top had made many enemies along the way. His Name was Gus Tucci, and Tucci was an old-school thug. He had no intention of letting Tanner get away with killing a Made Man.

Eight weeks after O'Connell was wounded, Michael Waller came to visit him and Eloise. He was staying in Chicago, after having satisfied himself that O'Connell was past the risk of infection and on the mend.

The three of them sat around the kitchen table with cups of coffee, as Waller pointed out the huge classified ad in the center of the page.

TANNER. ALL IS FORGIVEN. CALL THE USUAL NUMBER AND LET'S TALK. LUMPY AIELLO SAYS HELLO.

O'CONNELL SIGHED. WHOEVER HAD PLACED THE AD WAS telling him that they had a man named Lumpy Aiello with them. Aiello got the nickname Lumpy back in 1917, after

O'Connell had shoved him down a flight of stairs along with another man. The resultant fall had left Aiello with a huge bump on his forehead.

"You know this man, Aiello?" Waller asked.

"Yes, and he knows what I look like. That means they'll have him nearby until they're sure they have me in whatever trap they're setting."

"What's the usual number?" Eloise asked.

"I assume it's the same number I used to call Jimmy Maloney at his bar."

"Don't call it, Keane," Eloise begged. "You're retired, remember? You said that you would retire."

O'Connell jabbed a stiff finger against the ad and spoke in an angry tone. "This ad was placed by a man named Gus Tucci. Tucci is calling Tanner out publicly. If I don't respond, they'll assume they no longer have to fear me."

"They don't have to fear you," Eloise said. "You're done with work. You said that you would retire. Are you going back on your word?"

O'Connell sighed in frustration, as conflicting desires battled within him. He wanted to retire, but he couldn't stand the thought of Tanner's reputation being sullied. If Tanner failed to respond to such an obvious challenge, it would be tantamount to displaying cowardice. He had not spent over two decades creating the legend of Tanner just to have it die an ignominious death.

"Maybe they just want to talk," O'Connell said, but there was no conviction in his voice.

Eloise slid her chair closer and put her arms around him. "I don't want you to meet with anyone, and you yourself said it would be a trap."

O'Connell kissed her cheek. "I don't want to go either."

"Then don't go. I can't lose you, Keane. I can't."

There was silence in the kitchen. It was only interrupted by the humming sound made by the new contraption O'Connell had surprised Eloise with, a refrigerator.

Waller spoke first. "Could you dictate the terms of the meeting, Keane?"

"Maybe, why?"

Waller grinned. "I have an idea."

THE CHANGING OF THE GUARD

Tanner contacted Gus Tucci and agreed to meet in the village of Thornton, Illinois, which was just south of Chicago. They would meet inside a quarry early on a Sunday morning when the business was closed and most of the residents around them would be asleep.

Tanner knew it was a trap and that he was risking much, but he also had faith in the plan devised by Michael Waller. He checked his watch when he saw three cars drive through the gates at the quarry's entrance. Tucci was an hour early. On the phone, Tucci had told him that he would arrive with only three men, but apparently, that was a lie. Tanner had arrived early as well, for he was too wise to ever trust a man like Tucci.

One of the cars stayed at the gate and four men got out of it. They were all holding weapons, but they were revolvers. Given the distance, their guns weren't a threat. They were there to keep Tanner from driving away.

Tanner stood in the center of the wide quarry, which had been in operation for years. The other two cars parked a short distance away, and seven men climbed out. One of the men was Lumpy Aiello. Aiello had run the numbers racket for Recti and hadn't been a street soldier for years. He was a few years younger than O'Connell but hadn't aged well. He had a gut, was balding, and wore thick glasses.

With his right hand, Tanner was holding a Tommy gun with the barrel pointed at the ground. In his left hand was a box. The box had an antenna sticking out of it and several switches on top. Two of Tucci's men also had Thompson submachine guns, while the rest carried revolvers. They approached Tanner slowly, their guns lowered, their eyes watchful.

Tucci carried no weapon, nor did Lumpy Aiello. They stayed behind the other men, using them as a shield. When they were thirty feet apart, Tanner spoke.

"You told me you'd only bring two men with you, Tucci."

Tucci smiled, revealing straight white teeth. "I lied," Tucci said, then he spoke to Lumpy. "Is that Tanner?"

Lumpy stepped around one of Tucci's men to get a better look and a bullet shattered his glasses. The slug obliterated Aiello's right eye and blew out the back of his head. The shocking sight of his death was followed by the boom of a rifle echoing off the walls of the quarry.

"Anybody gets jumpy and Tucci dies next," Tanner said, and held up the box.

"Nobody shoots! Nobody shoots!" Tucci shouted, then pushed down the gun barrel of one man who wouldn't listen. When he turned back to look at Tanner, there was fury in his eyes.

"What the hell is that you're holding? Is that a bomb?"

"It's a device that controls things using radio waves. I've rigged it to work with a rifle. If my thumb pushes the lever beneath it, the rifle will fire at you."

"Bullshit!" Tucci said.

One of his men spoke up. He was in his forties and had a crooked nose. "Mr. Tucci, back when I was in the navy, they used these radio-controlled ships for artillery practice, and that was about fifteen years ago. Maybe he really did rig up a rifle to shoot."

"Could be," said another of the men. "I know a guy who got something like that to make his garage door go up and down just by pushing a button. It's the damnedest thing you've ever seen."

A third man looked as if he were trying to keep from laughing. He had a bushy black moustache and was standing at Tucci's left.

Tucci looked at the men who had spoken, then back at the box in Tanner's hand, before pointing at the body lying at his feet. "Lumpy Aiello was a Made Man too. Nobody touches a Made Man!"

"I do," Tanner said. "I'm not a member of your little club, your Outfit, or any other crime syndicate. I'm an independent. I killed Frank Recti because he threatened me. Would you like to be next, Tucci?"

"You're not getting out of here, Tanner. Just look around at how many men you're facing."

"I faced more men the night I killed Frank Recti. But we don't have to kill each other, Tucci. We would both be better off if we worked together. From what I hear, you've got enemies of your own. Pay me what I ask, and I'll kill them for you."

Tucci was quiet, as he seemed to be considering Tanner's offer, but then he shook his head. "It's no deal. I —" Tucci stopped speaking as he noticed the man on his left raise his gun. It was the man with the bushy moustache. An instant later, and the man shot Tucci in his open mouth. Then, two of Tucci's other men shot the men who were standing beside them.

Tanner eased his finger off the machine gun's trigger, as he had nearly blasted all of them.

The man who had killed Tucci ordered the other two men to start loading the bodies into the cars. He then holstered his gun and grinned at Tanner.

"I'm Mike Scalia, Tanner. I'll take that deal you offered Tucci."

Tanner cocked his head. "This was all sanctioned by the council, wasn't it?"

"It was, and my uncle just happens to sit on that council."

Tanner glanced back at the gate. The vehicle that had been blocking it was gone.

"I own a restaurant on State Street named Angelo's," Scalia said. "Call me there tomorrow and we'll work out a system like you had before. A guy like you, I'm betting you don't want too many people to know what you look like."

"You're right."

Mike Scalia stared past Tanner, to the open window of the quarry's office. When he spoke, there was a small smile playing on his lips.

"A radio wave controlled rifle, huh?"

"That's what I said. Why, do you doubt that I'm Tanner?"

"Hey, pally, no one but Tanner would have had the guts to show up here. Give me that call, let's say five o'clock?"

"I'll call," Tanner said.

Mike Scalia and his two men took off a few moments later. They had bodies to bury.

Tanner strode toward the office, as Keane O'Connell

walked out of the small building holding a rifle with a scope attached.

"Did they buy our ruse, Michael?"

"They did," Waller said. He was brushing his fingers across his temples, removing the white powder he'd placed there to make himself appear older. "The hardest part was remembering to talk with an Irish accent."

O'Connell laid a hand on Michael Waller's shoulder. "You've done it now, lad. There's no turning back. From here on out, you're Tanner."

"I know, and I promise that I'll use the same rules that you did when you were Tanner."

They climbed into the car they used and drove out the exit. There were a few people coming to investigate the gunfire, but they were on foot and too far away to get a good look inside the car.

ONCE THEY WERE BACK IN CHICAGO, O'CONNELL CALLED Eloise and let her know that all was well, and that he was returning to her in one piece. They had parked their own cars at the train station. After O'Connell finished his call home, he joined Waller by the vehicles and held out his hand.

"Good luck, Michael. Being an assassin is not the worst life a man can have, but you'll have to watch your back at every turn."

"I'll make you proud, Keane. The name Tanner is respected. I'll make sure it stays respected."

O'Connell had been shaking Waller's hand. He stopped shaking and gave it a firm squeeze. "Goodbye, lad, and don't be a stranger."

Keane O'Connell watched Michael Waller drive off,

watched Tanner drive off, and felt a strange mix of emotions. He was no longer Tanner, and yet, Tanner still existed. It was the nearest thing to having a son he'd felt since his own child had died as a baby.

O'Connell left the train station to head off to a life of leisure, of quiet study, and of peace.

MORE THAN CURIOSITY

As the sun was setting, Tanner and Romeo heard from Spenser, who told them he had handled the problem of the Greene brothers. He was coming to the house to see Andrea, to assure her that Tricks was safe, and would stay out of her life.

Tanner had spent the early evening thinking about the events that had occurred at the abandoned store. Whatever the phony Reverend and his men were up to, it wasn't good. Tanner was also intrigued by Ethan's tale of a disappearing truck.

With Spenser still on his way to the house, Tanner informed Romeo that he was going to check out the store.

"I'll come with you," Romeo said.

"No, I'll check it out alone. If I bite off more than I can chew, then you and Spenser can come and help me."

Romeo laughed. "More than *you* can chew? Bro, if you had been a Spartan fighting the Persians, that movie about the battle wouldn't have been named 300, it would've been called 1."

"I still don't know what's going on there. It may be

nothing, or all hell could break loose. It'll be good to know I can count on you to come and pluck me out of the fire."

"Hell yeah, and if you're not back by the time Spenser gets here, then we'll come find you."

"It sounds like a plan," Tanner said.

TANNER REACHED THE STORE, THEN WALKED AROUND THE building. There were no lights on inside and the parking lot was dark and devoid of vehicles. The moon overhead was just a crescent, but it gave off enough light to navigate by once your eyesight became adjusted.

Tanner moved toward the building. He wore a bandana over the bottom half of his face to hinder being identified, while a baseball cap hid his eyes in shadow. He saw no signs of cameras but understood well that they could be concealed. Ignoring the front doors, Tanner returned to the spot where Ethan said the truck he'd seen had disappeared.

The dumpster was still there. When Tanner looked inside it, he saw a jumble of old signage from the store that had once occupied the building, along with discarded merchandise displays.

When he moved behind the dumpster to examine the brick wall, he received a surprise. There was threaded rod at the bottom of the wall connected to the base of the dumpster, while the brick surrounding the rods was fake and a type of simulated brick wallpaper.

Tanner used his right hand and felt along the wall. Within moments he detected a zigzagging seam in the brick. The seam was lined up within the mortar. Tanner had no crowbar, but he had taken a tire iron from his trunk before leaving the house. After several minutes of effort, he managed to wedge the tool in the seam. When he attempted to widen the gap, the tool slipped through and struck something, which caused a spark. Tanner was shoved backwards violently as the dumpster and the wall rolled aside with great speed.

Tanner had also heard a sound before the noise of the moving wall had eclipsed it. It was a whooshing sound. He understood that he had somehow activated the airbags that were used to power the hidden opening into the building. Or rather, he had damaged one airbag, while activating the other, because the dumpster had failed to move more than six feet.

He waited a moment, listening for any sounds of movement or voices. He heard neither, but the faint sound of machinery drifted up from below. Tanner shone a flashlight into the darkness while keeping his body behind cover. Nothing happened, but his beam revealed a concrete ramp that showed signs of much use.

He understood then. He was looking at a ramp that led down to an underground loading dock. Some older retail buildings had them, and apparently, this was one such building. After attempting in vain to move the dumpster and widen the gap, Tanner gazed down into the underground passage and saw that it curved out of view.

He took a step inside, but then hesitated. He was not out to fulfill a contract and his business in the town was finished. Once Spenser spoke to Andrea, he and Romeo could trail along behind Spenser and return to Spenser's home. He was on an overdue vacation, spending time with friends and family. What was he doing exploring hidden underground chambers? There was no sense risking himself just to appease his curiosity.

Then, he thought about Ethan. The men he'd seen earlier had gotten a good look at the boy. If they decided that he knew something he shouldn't, they might harm the kid, and perhaps Andrea and Jasmine as well.

Tanner moved the flashlight to his left hand, then took out his gun and headed down the ramp. If there was trouble, he'd handle it, just like he always had.

~

BACK AT SPENSER'S HOUSE, AMY HAD RECEIVED A CALL from Spenser telling her that they would all be back later that night. After hanging up, Amy decided to cook something for dinner, and both Sara and Nadya agreed to help her. The women had watched their fourth Drake Diamond video and had started on their third bottle of wine.

The baby woke up again, and so they decided to play music to soothe her. Soon after, the kitchen filled with the aroma of food and laughter.

~

AS TANNER MOVED DEEPER ALONG THE WINDING underground loading dock ramp, the sound of machinery grew more distinct. It was a high-pitched noise. There was light as well, and it grew brighter as Tanner neared the bottom. The noise he heard was coming from a solar inverter which was behind a four-foot-high enclosure made of chain link fencing. There were also storage batteries lined up.

Tanner found the white straight truck that Ethan had seen earlier. It was parked at the loading dock at the end of the tunnel. There were no keys in the cab, but the rear of the truck was loaded with what Tanner assumed were stolen goods.

There were an assortment of TV's, cameras, and computers. None of it looked new, yet it could bring a price on the streets. A collection of firearms had been wrapped in a blanket, among them a pump-action shotgun which was clean and fully loaded. Tanner left the truck but carried the shotgun with him.

As Tanner walked by what had once been a glass-enclosed office for the security guards who manned the loading dock, he saw three monitors. All three showed different angles of the parking lot, including the gaping entry to the underground dock. He wondered where the cameras were hidden and decided to remove the DVD from the machine that was recording the video.

The parking lot was still empty, and so Tanner stayed a while to explore. He came across more stolen goods, but this batch was sitting on a wooden pallet and wrapped with plastic.

A huge cardboard box held movies, game, and music discs, while another one was half-filled with name-brand celebrity footwear. Tanner chuckled as he realized what he'd stumbled upon.

The good Reverend Smith and his friends were part of a home invasion team, and they were using the abandoned store as a base. Given the amount of stolen goods, they were either prolific or had many members. Perhaps they were even a gang.

Having seen enough, Tanner decided to leave the way he'd entered. Once he returned to Andrea's home, he would make an anonymous call to the police. He normally would have minded his own business, but Ethan had been seen by the gang. Once they discovered that someone had broken in, they might think he was involved. It was better to let the police find the goods and deal with the crooks.

Movement on the monitors caught Tanner's eye as he

was walking past them on his way out. Several men were entering the building through the front door, maybe as many as ten. Tanner couldn't be certain they were all armed, but at least two of them held rifles.

He leapt off the edge of the loading dock and moved up the winding concrete ramp with the shotgun he had taken leading the way. The squeal of tires reached his ears as two pickup trucks parked at the top of the ramp, where the dumpster entrance sat half open. Those sounds were followed by the opening and closing of the vehicles' doors, and a shouted command.

"Jake, Reno, you two stay here. If the bastard shows himself, shoot him."

Then came the sound of footsteps as a group ran toward Tanner along the ramp. He turned to head back inside and make his way up to the sales floor, where there had to be numerous exits. He was headed for the dock again when loud voices drifted down from the stairs located near the security office, the voices were accompanied by the distinct sound of a shotgun being racked.

When he turned and looked along the sloping concrete dock, Tanner saw the shadows of six men playing along the wall and growing larger, they too were holding guns. He was trapped, outnumbered, and out-gunned.

Tanner looked around at his surroundings while remaining calm. He was a Tanner. The seventh Tanner, and he had trained for and survived dangerous situations in the past. The men headed toward him were angry and filled with the desire to kill, but Tanner knew something that they didn't. Many, if not all of them were going to die.

"There he is!" cried a deep male voice from behind him.

Tanner raised the shotgun and fired.

26

FUTURE'S PAST

THE OUTSKIRTS OF CHICAGO, JULY 1951

Michael Waller, Tanner Two, drove along a road he hadn't been on for nearly a decade. During his absence, several new homes had gone up in the area. However, he was pleased to see that the house he was headed to still sat alone amid its own acreage.

Waller was driving a red Cadillac convertible, A Series 62, and its whitewall tires gleamed in the sun.

The house looked the same as he remembered it, but the gravel driveway was paved and bordered by colorful wildflowers. There was a car in the driveway that he'd never seen before, a huge black Buick. Like his own vehicle, it was a convertible.

Waller walked up the front steps of the porch, but as he raised his hand to ring the doorbell, he sensed that someone had come up behind him. Someone he hadn't heard at all.

"Hello, lad."

Waller smiled as he turned around, and there stood Keane O'Connell. The sixty-seven-year-old O'Connell's hair was stark white but had lost none of its thickness. His friend seemed smaller to Waller than he remembered, but he still looked fit. O'Connell's casual gray slacks and blue corduroy shirt had streaks of fresh soil on them, and he held a pair of gardening gloves in his left hand.

The two men shook hands, then shared a quick hug. As they were separating, Eloise stepped out onto the porch. Waller thought she looked as beautiful as ever, although there were lines about her eyes and silver streaks in her hair. But then, none of them was getting any younger.

WALLER JOINED THEM FOR DINNER AND DECIDED TO STAY the night as well, after Eloise insisted that he not drive back to Detroit in the dark. Michael Waller had moved to Detroit in 1942, and as it had been in Chicago, the name Tanner was legendary among those in the Detroit underworld, legendary, respected, and feared.

After eating a large breakfast, O'Connell led Waller outside to look at his flower and vegetable garden. Over the years, he had become quite the horticulturist.

Eloise kissed Waller goodbye, as she was headed off to her volunteer job at the library. She made Waller promise to bring his lady friend along the next time he visited. Waller was living with a woman who had become widowed during World War Two. He'd told O'Connell and Eloise that he had plans to marry her.

Earlier that morning, O'Connell had set a large book on the patio table. The book had hundreds of pages, most of which were blank. Eloise had brought it home from the library. The book was leather-bound, but had no title or other markings, and its pages were blank.

It had been in a shipment of dictionaries and was obviously sent out in error from the printer. Eloise asked if she could have it, then gave it to O'Connell.

"Why give it to me?" O'Connell had asked her.

"You've led an interesting life. You should write your memoirs."

O'Connell had chuckled at that. "They wouldn't be memoirs. In the hands of the law, they'd be a confession."

Still, the idea had been planted. During the previous winter, with his garden dormant, Keane O'Connell began writing in the book. When he had finished months later, he had written down not only a memoir about his life, but had also penned his philosophy, along with strategies and tricks he had developed while acting as Tanner.

As they sat by the garden under the patio umbrella, Michael Waller scanned the book with fascinated eyes. When he was done, he sat the fledgling tome upon the table and looked over at O'Connell.

"Eloise was right to suggest you write this. I think I'll do the same someday."

O'Connell pointed at the book. "I've barely made a dent in those pages. You could begin penning your story where mine ends."

Waller stared at the book, then nodded in agreement at the idea. After taking a sip of the iced tea they were enjoying, Waller gave O'Connell some news.

"I'm thinking of retiring after I've married. I've also become friends with a young man who would make an excellent Tanner."

O'Connell raised his eyebrows in surprise at both statements.

"Are you retiring because of your coming marriage?"

"Partly, but I'm not a young man anymore, Keane. I'll be fifty next year."

"Fifty?" O'Connell whispered in surprise. It seemed like only a few years ago that he'd met Waller, the fearless lad who had lied about his age so that he could go to war and find adventure.

Waller lifted the book from the table, to flip through it once more. It was the book that would become known as the Book of Tanner.

O'Connell took off his reading glasses and put them back in their leather case. Then, he asked a question. "This fellow you've befriended, what's he like?"

"He's as brave and foolish as we were at his age, but smart too, and like me, he went to war young, then saw action in the Pacific during World War Two."

"Was he a sniper?"

"No, but I've been training him and he's a hell of a marksman. I've taught him the tricks you taught me, and a few others I developed on my own. Like myself, he'll abide by the code you developed."

"What about the transition from one Tanner to the next, how will you handle that?"

"He's a Cajun and wants to go back home. He'll be working in the New Orleans area."

"A third Tanner," O'Connell said. "It makes me wonder if there will be a fourth someday."

"And then a fifth, perhaps a sixth?" Waller said. "And with each man gaining the experience and guidance of the Tanners who came before him. If that ever happened, imagine what such a man would be like."

O'Connell did imagine it, and he smiled at the thought. "Such a man would be unbeatable, no matter the odds he faced."

27

UNBEATABLE

WITH GROUPS OF ARMED MEN CLOSING IN ON HIM FROM each end of the underground loading dock, Tanner raised his shotgun and fired. He wasn't firing at the men headed toward him. He was destroying their source of light.

Tanner sent three blasts into the storage batteries and the solar inverter, then dived to the floor. Darkness enveloped the space he was in, then was interrupted by bright flashes as the men expended rounds. They were firing at the spot where Tanner had been standing, and so missed him.

Tanner fired the last two shells in the shotgun toward the flashes he'd seen. Screams of pain erupted, but Tanner barely heard them as he released the shotgun and rolled to where he recalled the truck was.

The men on the ramp had made it all the way down to the dock and were greeted by panicked fire from their comrades who were standing by the security office.

"Don't shoot! We'll hit each other."

Tanner recognized the voice that had uttered those words. It was Reverend Smith.

"Use your phones like a flashlight," another voice said.

As the men began activating their phones, Tanner moved silently toward the group that had come down the ramp. Like himself, they wore ski masks or bandanas. They had no desire to have their faces filmed inside a warehouse of stolen goods and had yet to determine who had broken into their lair. Tanner stood among them with his phone held out in front of him, just as they were doing, blending in.

Three wounded men were on the floor. One was gritting his teeth from the pain in his right arm, which had been wounded by shotgun pellets, another man moaned while lying flat on his back, and the third man looked crumpled and dead.

"Shit! Who got killed?" said a voice on Tanner's right.

One of the men bent down with his phone, turned the man over, and lifted a ski mask.

"It's Maury. The son of a bitch killed Maury."

The Reverend spoke up again, but Tanner still couldn't make him out. He was just a shadow behind the bright screen of his phone.

"Form groups of two and search the dock. He must be hiding here somewhere."

"Maybe we killed him already," another man said. He was a large man, tall and wide, and he held a rifle with a thirty-round magazine.

Tanner eased toward him while removing his knife and saw the man's phone screen fade to darkness. It was a cheap phone and the screen had already timed-out once before. "We need flashlights," the big man said.

"Use the App on your phone," a voice said.

"I don't have a fucking App," the big man growled.

While the men had been talking, Tanner had put away his phone. He stepped behind the big man, gripped the back of his shirt, then thrust his blade into the base of the giant's spine.

∾

Spenser had arrived at Andrea's home at the same time Tanner was inspecting the truck full of stolen goods. When Romeo told him where Tanner had gone, and why, Spenser smiled.

"That boy attracts trouble," Spenser said, but after looking around he had a question for Andrea. "Where's Ethan?"

∾

Ethan used Spenser's arrival at the house as an opportunity to sneak out the back door. He knew Tanner was at the store looking around, and he wanted in on the excitement. The truck he'd seen earlier had just vanished, and the mystery had been on Ethan's mind all day. When Tanner figured out how it was done, he wanted to be there to see it.

Ethan walked out from among a group of trees and the store came into view. There were cars and trucks parked near the front entrance, which meant that Tanner may have been caught sneaking around. Ethan stayed to the shadows along the border of the parking lot and made his way around to the rear.

Two more trucks were there, along with two men wearing masks standing by the dumpster. Ethan smiled when he saw that there was a hidden entrance sitting ajar. That was where the truck had gone earlier, and he was sure that Tanner had found the opening.

Ethan moved toward the entrance by walking on an

angle that kept him hidden from sight behind the pickup trucks. He nearly cried out when the sound of shotgun blasts drifted out of the opening. That was followed by the sound of more shots from different guns, and then there was silence.

"Tanner?" Ethan whispered and wondered if the man had been shot for trespassing. His body began to shake from fear, and he turned to head back the way he'd come. He was so rattled that he wasn't paying attention and his foot kicked an empty soda can.

The men at the door spotted him running away, and one of them gave chase. He was a youthful figure with long legs, and he was eating up the ground between himself and Ethan.

Tears ran down Ethan's face as he raced toward home, and the sound of the footfalls behind him grew louder and louder.

THE MAN WHOSE SPINE TANNER HAD SEVERED LET OUT A high-pitched scream and dropped to his knees.

Tanner released the knife and gained possession of the rifle. He thumbed off the safety and fired at the men closest to him.

Panic erupted, phones were fumbled, then dropped, and men fired in his direction. Tanner had taken cover behind the man he had knifed and felt two rounds strike the man's thick body.

"Damn it. Stop firing!" a voice cried out, the voice of the phony reverend. Tanner eased the rifle around the body of the man he was propping up and fired several rounds toward the voice. A shout of pain erupted, followed by the sound of running feet. The men were retreating toward the stairs.

Tanner let loose another burst and again heard screams of pain. Another round hit the man he was holding, and the man's head slumped forward until his chin rested on his massive chest. He released his grip on the man and crawled along the base of the wall. Concrete rained down on him as scattered shots hit the wall of the ramp.

When Tanner was certain he had moved around a curve and out of range, he stood and listened. He heard moans, curses, cries of agony, and sobs of sorrow. What he didn't hear was the sound of footfalls approaching from the surface. The men guarding the exit had stayed in place.

Tanner headed up the ramp, bathed in darkness, and ready to kill once more.

"Stop running, you little shit, or I'll shoot your ass."

Ethan looked back and saw that the man with the gun was reaching out to grab him. A finger grazed his shoulder. It was followed by a hand, and the hand grabbed onto his collar. Ethan tried to twist free and only managed to trip himself up. He fell forward, his palms scraping the rough surface of the parking lot and sending a jolt of stinging pain through both hands.

Terror erased the pain as Ethan flipped over onto his back and started slapping and kicking at the man, who had bent over to grab him. When his hand touched the ski mask the man wore, he gripped it and yanked it off the man's head. The man beneath the mask was young and had his blond hair in a buzz cut.

"I didn't do anything!" Ethan said, as tears rolled down his cheeks.

The man lifted Ethan, until the boy was on his knees. "You've seen my face. That's bad enough, kid."

The man smiled as he took out a knife with a razor-sharp edge. He was pulling on Ethan's hair, forcing his head back to expose his throat, and that's when a shot rang out from the shadows. The sick smile left the man's face.

Ethan fell to the ground along with the punk and watched as a spreading circle of red darkened the man's white shirt, where his heart would be.

The boy cried out in fright as a hand grabbed his arm to help him up. It was Romeo, wearing a bandana and a cap. Ethan understood that Romeo had just saved his life.

"That was a close call, little dude."

Spenser came up behind Romeo and tousled Ethan's hair. He was wearing a balaclava, his one good eye visible in the open slit of the fabric.

"Take him home to his mother," Spenser said.

"I'll be back in a flash," Romeo told him. He picked up a still tearful Ethan and carried him off toward home, while running.

TANNER HEARD A FAINT ECHO OF ROMEO'S SHOT WHEN HE was nearing the exit and wondered what it meant. He eased along the curving wall of the ramp while staying low, knowing that someone could be lying in wait around the next curve. He played it patient, listened and waited, then he heard a voice from outside.

"Drop your weapon."

Spenser, Tanner thought, as he recognized the voice of his mentor.

Whoever Spenser was speaking to didn't heed his advice because his words were followed by gunfire.

"Spenser, it's me," Tanner said, as he walked up the ramp and outside. After greeting each other and learning about Ethan, Tanner explained the situation.

"Judging by all the vehicles, I'd say that there were fifteen to twenty men involved. How many are left down there," Spenser asked.

"Half a dozen at most," Tanner said. "There was a lot of friendly fire going on once they panicked."

A car appeared. It was rocketing across the parking lot with its headlights off while weaving around the dormant light poles. Someone had covered the license plates with strips of duct tape.

As the vehicle neared, the dome light flashed on, then off, and they saw that Romeo was the driver.

The car braked to a hard stop beside them.

"Get in! Andrea got nervous and called the cops when she heard the shooting."

Spenser and Tanner climbed inside the car, with Tanner in the rear. Tanner had his rifle held steady on the frame of the rolled down window.

"Ethan told me about a way out of the lot that's on the south side," Romeo said. "There used to be a wooden fence blocking the street, but the fence fell down."

Tanner saw movement, as the glass doors of the store began opening. He fired off a string of shots and the doors shattered, as Romeo rocketed past the entrance.

"I see police lights reflecting off the trees," Spenser said. "They're coming in silent from the other side of the store."

Romeo found the spot that Ethan had told him about. He slowed, and the car thumped hard over a fallen hurricane fence.

They were on a side street that led out to the highway. Romeo pulled over and they watched as three more police cars sped toward the rear entrance of the store.

"Take us back to Andrea's," Spenser said.

"Aye, aye, Captain," Romeo said.

Tanner's phone vibrated. It was Sara.

"Will you guys be home soon? We cooked and figured we could have a late dinner."

"It might be more than an hour, but we'll be home tonight."

"Goody."

"Goody?"

Sara giggled and said, "I missed you today." It came out sounding like "I mished you todaz."

"I missed you too," Tanner said, and in the background, he heard Amy and Nadya giggling about something.

When the call ended, Tanner made an observation. "I think our women are drunk."

"Nothing wrong with that," Romeo said. "Drunk women are horny women."

ANDREA AND JASMINE WERE GLAD TO SEE THEM RETURN, while Ethan gave Romeo a hug. From an upstairs window, the parking lot of the abandoned store looked like a police convention was taking place, and there were numerous ambulances sprinkled in among the cop cars.

"They'll send someone to follow up on the call you made reporting that you heard shots," Spenser told Andrea. "But remember, we were never here."

"I won't say a word," Andrea said. "And thank you again, Spenser."

The three men got into their cars and headed for Spenser's home. They had a vacation to get back to.

28

IT WOULDN'T BE A PARTY WITHOUT THEM

TANNER TWISTED THE THROTTLE OF THE BIG HARLEY HE was riding and gained enough speed to move past Spenser.

Amy held onto Spenser with her arms locked around his waist, the same way that Sara was holding onto Tanner. Both Tanner and Spenser were losing the race, because Romeo and Nadya were tearing up the track. Up ahead, Romeo made the final turn at high speed while counter steering. Romeo's Harley leaned over so far that his knee nearly touched the ground.

The skillful maneuver increased Romeo's lead, causing Tanner to laugh. He had never beaten his friend in a race during the days they had traveled the southwest together, and it looked like nothing had changed. Romeo won the race, with Tanner coming in second and Spenser a heartbeat behind him.

As Tanner brought the bike to rest, Sara ripped her helmet off and smiled at him. "That was such a rush."

They had borrowed three of four available motorcycles from Spenser's guests, who were there for a party. The young men's names were Johnny, Lionel, Eddie, and Sean, but they went by their nicknames of Scar, Abrasion, Bruise, and Wound. They were the Tin Horsemen.

Scar and the other horsemen played a role in Tanner's victory over Alonso Alvarado. They had been mercenaries seeking to claim the price that had been on Tanner's head. After Scar realized that Spenser was the man who had helped his mother years earlier, the Tin Horsemen switched sides. They had even come away from the adventure with money in their pockets, thanks to a ruse played on Alvarado.

Abrasion had a girlfriend named Deedee. Deedee was also a friend and employee of Amy's and worked at the store in town that Amy owned with her brother.

Deedee carried baby Florentina to her parents as Romeo and Nadya got off Abrasion's bike.

"That was some kind of awesome, Romeo," Abrasion said.

"Thanks, dude. It's been a long time since I rode a Harley this big."

As Abrasion rolled his bike over to rejoin Deedee, Tanner and Spenser walked over and congratulated Romeo on his win, while Sara, Amy, and Nadya discussed the ride.

They had raced along a two-mile track that was normally used for running. Romeo had gained the lead from Tanner on the third and final lap, and never gave it back.

Romeo walked over to see his daughter, leaving Tanner and Spenser alone. Spenser gestured over at the Tin Horsemen, who were hanging out under a tree and drinking beer.

"Remember when they were just a group of directionless boys?"

Tanner looked the biker gang over. "Yeah, and now they're a group of directionless men."

Sara walked over with Amy. Both women were smiling. Amy had grown to like Sara, and they found that they had similar tastes in books and movies.

Tanner and Sara had stayed at Spenser's home for two weeks, and the time had gone by quickly, but they had plans to fly back to New York City within a few days.

Back home in Manhattan, their new apartment was being remodeled during their absence. The construction company handling the renovation was secretly owned by the Giacconi Family. One new addition to the condo would be a carefully concealed gun safe, and it would be fully stocked.

Sara fell into Tanner's arms and gazed up at him. "I'm glad we came here, and I loved getting to know your family."

"What about your family?"

Sara made a worried face. "Maybe someday, my father can be difficult."

"Whenever you're ready. Besides, I'm still getting used to us."

Sara laughed. "I know what you mean. I still marvel at the fact that we're together. But we're good together, and I'm as happy as I've ever been."

Tanner kissed her. "It's working on my end."

Nadya walked over and handed Florentina to Sara. The baby was crying softly as she fought sleep.

"Sing that song again, Sara," Nadya said. "Florentina likes it."

Sara began singing a lullaby to the drowsy baby. Florentina's eyes closed within moments.

Nadya whispered to Sara as she took back her baby. "You have to teach me that song before you leave."

"I'll do that," Sara said softly.

"What was that you sang?" Tanner asked.

"Its name is, *All the Pretty Little Horses*. I've also heard it called, *Hush a Bye*. My mother used to sing it to me."

Tanner had a faraway look in his eyes. "My mother sang it to me when I was little, although I'd forgotten that memory until you sang the song."

Sara smiled up at him. "You're different here."

"In what way?"

"You're more Cody than Tanner here."

"I've had to be Tanner for most of my adult life. There was no Cody Parker to go back to. As far as the world is concerned, Cody Parker is dead."

"I've never realized that," Sara said. "Spenser and the other Tanners could carry out an assassination and go home to their lives, their pasts and true identities, but not you."

"No, not me."

"I want our home in New York to be that for you, to be a place where you can be yourself."

"Myself, and not Tanner?"

"Yes."

"Sara, I'm not sure I even know who that is."

29

HOMAGE

As Tanner and Sara prepared to leave for Manhattan, hugs and kisses were exchanged all around, as well as promises to get together again soon.

Romeo, Nadya, and the baby weren't leaving until the following day, and so Tanner and Sara were making the trip to the airport alone. After the goodbyes had been exchanged, Spenser walked Tanner and Sara out to their car.

"You're sure you don't want me to tag along behind and see you two off, boy?" Spenser asked Tanner.

"No, Spenser, we're good, there's no point in you driving back and forth to the airport."

Spenser hugged Tanner. "Take care of yourself, Cody. I'm so damn proud of you."

"I owe my life to you, Spenser. I never forget that."

Tanner and Sara arrived at the airport a short time later. They both felt revitalized by the relaxing time they'd enjoyed at Spenser's home. When they learned that their flight had been cancelled and that they would have a three hour wait, Tanner turned to Sara.

"Are you in a hurry to get back to Manhattan?"

"I suppose not, why?"

"I'd like to make a side trip. There's something I have to do, and it's something I should have done already."

~

ROSEHILL CEMETERY, CHICAGO, PRESENT DAY

As Sara watched from a stone bench, Tanner knelt and laid a wreath on the grave of Keane O'Connell. Afterward, he stood and stared down at the final resting place of O'Connell, as he thought about what the remarkable man had meant for his life.

If O'Connell had never become Tanner, had never passed along the title, handing it down through the years until it reached Spenser, a boy named Cody Parker would have died at the age of sixteen.

"Thank you, Keane O'Connell," Tanner said, and once again he read the simple headstone.

KEANE O'CONNELL
November 2, 1884 – July 30, 1967
HE WAS THE FIRST OF THE BEST

TANNER RETURNS!

REVELATIONS - BOOK 20

AFTERWORD

Thank you,

REMINGTON KANE

JOIN MY INNER CIRCLE

You'll receive FREE books, such as,

SLAY BELLS – A TANNER NOVEL – BOOK 0

TAKEN! ALPHABET SERIES – 26 ORIGINAL TAKEN! TALES

BLUE STEELE - KARMA

Also – Exclusive short stories featuring TANNER, along with other books.

TO BECOME AN INNER CIRCLE MEMBER, GO TO:
   http://remingtonkane.com/mailing-list/

ALSO BY REMINGTON KANE

The TANNER Series in order

The Young Guns Series in order

YOUNG GUNS

YOUNG GUNS 2 - SMOKE & MIRRORS

YOUNG GUNS 3 - BEYOND LIMITS

YOUNG GUNS 4 - RYKER'S RAIDERS

YOUNG GUNS 5 - ULTIMATE TRAINING

YOUNG GUNS 6 - CONTRACT TO KILL

YOUNG GUNS 7 - FIRST LOVE

YOUNG GUNS 8 - THE END OF THE BEGINNING

A Tanner Series in order

TANNER: YEAR ONE

TANNER: YEAR TWO

TANNER: YEAR THREE

TANNER: YEAR FOUR

TANNER: YEAR FIVE

The TAKEN! Series in order

TAKEN! - LOVE CONQUERS ALL - Book 1

TAKEN! - SECRETS & LIES - Book 2

TAKEN! - STALKER - Book 3

TAKEN! - BREAKOUT! - Book 4

TAKEN! - THE THIRTY-NINE - Book 5

TAKEN! - KIDNAPPING THE DEVIL - Book 6

TAKEN! - HIT SQUAD - Book 7

TAKEN! - MASQUERADE - Book 8

The MR. WHITE Series

The BLUE STEELE Series in order

BLUE STEELE - DADDY'S GIRL - Book 7 & the Series Finale

The CALIBER DETECTIVE AGENCY Series in order

CALIBER DETECTIVE AGENCY - GENERATIONS-
Book 1

CALIBER DETECTIVE AGENCY - TEMPTATION- Book 2

CALIBER DETECTIVE AGENCY - A RANSOM PAID IN
BLOOD- Book 3

CALIBER DETECTIVE AGENCY - MISSING- Book 4

CALIBER DETECTIVE AGENCY - DECEPTION- Book 5

CALIBER DETECTIVE AGENCY - CRUCIBLE- Book 6

CALIBER DETECTIVE AGENCY – LEGENDARY – Book 7

CALIBER DETECTIVE AGENCY – WE ARE GATHERED
HERE TODAY - Book 8

CALIBER DETECTIVE AGENCY - MEANS, MOTIVE, and
OPPORTUNITY - Book 9 & the Series Finale

THE TAKEN!/TANNER Series in order

THE CONTRACT: KILL JESSICA WHITE - Taken!/Tanner
- Book 1

UNFINISHED BUSINESS – Taken!/Tanner – Book 2

THE ABDUCTION OF THOMAS LAWSON -
Taken!/Tanner – Book 3

PREDATOR - Taken!/Tanner - Book 4

DETECTIVE PIERCE Series in order

MONSTERS - A Detective Pierce Novel - Book 1

DEMONS - A Detective Pierce Novel - Book 2

ANGELS - A Detective Pierce Novel - Book 3

THE OCEAN BEACH ISLAND Series in order

THE MANY AND THE ONE - Book 1

SINS & SECOND CHANES - Book 2

DRY ADULTERY, WET AMBITION -Book 3

OF TONGUE AND PEN - Book 4

ALL GOOD THINGS… - Book 5

LITTLE WHITE SINS - Book 6

THE LIGHT OF DARKNESS - Book 7

STERN ISLAND - Book 8 & the Series Finale

THE REVENGE Series in order

JOHNNY REVENGE - The Revenge Series - Book 1

THE APPOINTMENT KILLER - The Revenge Series - Book 2

AN I FOR AN I - The Revenge Series - Book 3

ALSO

THE EFFECT: Reality is changing!

THE FIX-IT MAN: A Tale of True Love and Revenge

DOUBLE OR NOTHING

PARKER & KNIGHT

REDEMPTION: Someone's taken her

DESOLATION LAKE

TIME TRAVEL TALES & OTHER SHORT STORIES

Made in the USA
Monee, IL
06 March 2023

29300005R00121